The Tides Wait for Me

The Fold has stolen so much from us all. My own story is a very sad one. The corrupt Fold ravaged my solar system, leaving nothing, not a single atom, in their disastrous wake. I, standing in solidarity with you here today, am all that is left of a once prosperous and peaceful interplanetary civilization. To you, here on Earth, The Fold appears strong, invincible, but let me tell you, people of Earth, The Fold is failing in nearly every corner of The Galaxy.

THE TINKER & THE FOLD

Part III – The Javelin Divide

By Evan & Scott Gordon

Laguna Lantern Publishing Company

2

Published by:
Laguna Lantern Publishing Company
Laguna Niguel, CA 92677

USA * Canada * UK * Australia * India
China * Mexico * EU * South Africa

First published in the United States of America
by Laguna Lantern Publishing Company.

Laguna Lantern Publishing Co. ISBN 9781704128597

Printed in the United Stated of America

Acknowledgments

Thank you to everyone that has assisted us on our nearly eight-year journey to make The Tinker and The Fold series a reality. We appreciate all your support, letters, suggestions, and words of encouragement. Our readers have truly made our journey worthwhile! We'd also like to offer a very special thank you to Julie Scheina whose editorial support throughout multiple revisions has allowed us to take our characters and the universe they inhabit to a whole new level. Welcome to The Tinkerverse.

-   Evan and Scott Gordon, November 2019

"He who fights with monsters might take care lest he thereby become a monster. And when you gaze long into an abyss, the abyss gazes into you."

- Nietzsche

Chapter I
Road Less Traveled

"Paul, what's happening?"

"They found us!"

"How? We're in the middle of nowhere..."

"I don't know. Where's Maria?"

"I thought she was with you."

"Mama? Papa? There are men outside."

"Maria, sweetie, come here," Bella squatted down to meet her, "there's nothing to worry about. Those men just want to talk with your father for a minute."

Paul slowly closed the kitchen blinds. He turned to his wife of twelve years, and his eight-year-old daughter and said, "I need you both to listen to me very carefully. Maria, these men aren't here for me, they're here for you. You are a very special little girl, and we must never let them find you."

"What do you mean, Papa?"

"You know how sometimes when you think of something, that something happens?"

"Yes, Papa."

"The men outside would like you to think things for them. They would like you to help them get what they want even if it means hurting people, but don't worry, Blackbird, Papa has a plan."

He quickly crossed the room and pulled a large chest away from the wall. He lifted the rug and underneath it lay a beat-up and faded wooden panel.

"As a boy, my grandfather brought me and my brothers to this cabin every summer for fishing trips. Many years ago it was used by Moonshiners to smuggle alcohol into the States during Prohibition. There are tunnels running for miles in every direction under these woods. My brothers and I used to explore them for days on end. I need you both to go down there and hide. I'll open the hatch again once the coast is clear. If anything happens to me, the main tunnel heading in that direction," he pointed, "will lead you to a creek a half mile or so north of here and put you on the Canadian side of the border."

He jerked the round iron handle and the panel creaked open. A stairway descended into a black hole.

"Paul, what's gonna happen to us?"

"Bella, you and Maria will be safe down there. Take this flashlight."

"Why won't you come with us?"

"If I come down there, no one will be up here to pull the carpet back over the trapdoor. They'll catch us all. You must go! Now!"

The window above the kitchen sink exploded and sent glass spraying everywhere. A metal cylinder thumped onto the floor in front of them. White gas spewed out of it.

"Go! Now! Please!"

The thunder of footsteps on the front porch caused Paul to grab Bella and force her down through the hatch. He grabbed Maria, kissed her on her head, and lowered her down into Bella's arms."

"Know that I love you to the moon and back."

"Shmily," Maria smiled.

"Shmily, Blackbird," Paul smiled back as he closed the trapdoor, "please take care of your mother for me."

A deafening crash was followed by the rush of heavy boots. Harsh muffled voices shouted. Then the commotion settled down. Maria could hear her father talking with them, though she could not make out the words through the thick floorboards. The exchange continued for a few minutes. Then there was a single gunshot and a loud thud on the floor above her.

Maria cried out. Her mother covered her mouth and whispered into her ear, "It's time to go," as she switched on the flashlight and pulled Maria down into the dark passage.

Soon they came upon three backpacks, several more flashlights, and an assortment of supplies hanging from hooks along the wall. Bella picked up a backpack and handed it to Maria.

"Put this on," she whispered.

As Maria put her arm through the strap, a loud raucous ensued above them. Boots banged. Doors opened and closed in rapid succession. Furniture was dragged across the floor or tossed to the side.

"They're looking for the trapdoor!"

Bella threw the pack over her shoulder, handed Maria a flashlight, and the two of them bolted off into the inky darkness.

"Where are we going?"

"Wherever this tunnel leads, sweetie."

Light suddenly flooded into the passage behind them.

"Oh my God! They found the door! Keep running!"

"Sir, the girl and her mother went this way!" a voice shouted.

Bella and Maria barreled ahead as the growing chorus of military voices barked orders behind them.

Maria skidded to a halt, "wait, mom, what's this?"

"Maria, we have to keep going."

"It's from papa. 'If you're reading this, it means the bad men have found me and will find you, too, if you don't pull this lever. Love you, Blackbird. - Papa.'

"Pull the lever? What lever?" Bella exclaimed, "we can't stop, Maria! They're are right behind us."

"This lever," Maria pointed. She grabbed the handle with both hands and strained to pull it as hard as she could, but couldn't budge it, "Help me, mama, it's stuck."

Bella also grabbed the lever and the two of them hung from the large iron handle, but it was stuck.

"Sir, there they are!"

A sea of flashlights converged on them, and soldiers filled the passageway.

One of the soldiers spoke in a calm but authoritative voice, "Maam, I'm going to need for you to come down from there."

Bella lowered herself from the handle and pulled Maria down after her.

"Now put the girl down and step over to the side."

"Mama, don't!"

"Maam, I need you to put her down."

Maria turned her attention back to the iron lever protruding from the wall of the tunnel, and as she did, it slowly creaked downward.

"Get her to stop doing that!" the soldier demanded, as set of large iron doors opened and dumped a massive pile of rocks and debris into the tunnel.

A thick cloud of acrid dust engulfed the corridor. The soldiers, at least for the moment, were trapped on the other side of a thick stone barrier.

"Your father thought of everything, didn't he?" Bella sighed, "let's not let him down now. C'mon."

She took Maria's hand and in a soft voice said, "Maria, those rocks will slow those men down, but they'll never stop looking for you. We have to get far away from here. Somewhere they can never find you."

"Where, mama?"

"Let's start with the other end of this tunnel."

Chapter 2
A Grand Entrance

"Mr. President, the very existence of the IRON presents a formidable challenge to our campaign to join The Fold. They are at this very moment undermining all of the good work we are doing to comply with The Fold's mandates."

"With all due respect, Mr. Neninjer, we don't have any proof that the IRON exists, much less that it's undermining our efforts. In fact, according to our Fold representatives we are tracking well toward the compliance goals we've been given to date."

"Sir, we have credible evidence to the contrary. Instances of anti-Fold propaganda and fake news are beginning to trend across social media," Neninjer suggested, "though the general populace still favors Fold membership."

"Neninjer, are you basing your argument for the existence of the IRON entirely on a few crackpot social media posts?" President Montoya challenged.

"Let me give you an example of the kinds of fake news articles we're seeing. Here's one that was posted this morning: *Are you next on The Fold's buffet menu? Click here to find to find out!*' And how about this one: *Is your favorite celebrity secretly an Aaptuuan brainwasher?* Or, *10 Ways to Survive the Impending Aaptuuan Apocalypse. Act now, the end is near!* and *Your favorite colors will determine if you are an alien.*

"I'd like to think that the average citizen is intelligent enough to see through such tripe. Does anyone other than Neninjer feel that the IRON is a credible threat?"

"I do, sir," said a voice from the back of the room.

"Okay, Mitchell, what do you have?"

"Three days ago, one of our field agents posing as a subversive intercepted a handwritten note from someone claiming to be an IRON operative. The note simply reads: 'Prepare Savior Arrival 3232032 @ 1446.'

"What do you make of it?"

"Sir, we believe that 3232032 refers to March 23rd, 2032 and 1446 refers to 2:46pm."

"Mitchell, if that's correct, you're theorizing that whatever this event is, it occurs tomorrow afternoon. Assuming you're right, who or what is the Savior?"

"Intelligence reports we've gathered indicate that the Savior is an extraterrestrial being who stands in direct opposition to The Fold. Its stated goal is to equip The Iron with advanced technology for the purpose of driving The Fold out of our solar system. I suggest we implement Protocol XT aka Project XtraTerrestrial."

"Hold on. What you're telling us, Agent Mitchell, is that tomorrow at 2:46pm a heretofore unknown and hostile alien force will arrive on Earth?" Montoya pressed, "That is a very serious accusation. I'm not convinced a single piece of paper containing a cryptic message is enough to warrant the initiation of Protocol XT. Even if it were, we don't have enough time to deploy it effectively."

"What good is Protocol XT if they get here before we've had a chance to activate it?" Neninjer asked.

An intecom buzzer interrupted their debate and an image of General Fahd, head of the interstellar communication initiative for NASA, appeared on the wall opposite President Montoya.

"General Fahd, give me some good news."

"Mr. President, we've just received an inbound radio message from The Fold. They are sending a representative to Washington to meet with you, sir."

"That's odd. The Fold hasn't ever announced its visits in advance. General Fahd, did they mention when they'd be arriving?"

"Yes, sir. They will be landing on the White House lawn tomorrow at 2:46pm."

"Well... shit."

Chapter 3
A Dose of Enlightenment

Cyd tossed and turned on the rickety cot in the darkened stucco room.

"And so, the tinker unfolds!" Hazbog laughed maniacally, hurling Jett into the blood mist.

Hazbog then dove off the branch and plunged into the mist after him. A loud sonic pulse erupted, and the blood mist imploded in on itself. Hazbog, Nukii, Jett, and the blood mist were gone.

"Jett!" Cyd cried waving her disabled manipulation wand around frantically.

"What happened?" Jack yelled, "where'd they go?"

Le-Wa's voice came over Cyd's comm-link, "An enormous quantum disturbance has been detected. Our scans indicate no sign of Jett, Nukii, Hazbog, or the blood mist."

Then the scene suddenly shifted. Cyd found herself awash in the blood mist with Jett as he fought desperately to prevent it from choking the life out of him. The space behind Jett collapsed in on itself, a black swirling hole appeared. Out of the void stepped the lanky silhouette of a man with a broad brimmed hat and flowing black robe. In a single swift movement, the man snatched Jett and Nukii and pulled them back into the void. But before it vanished, the being's face lit up with a gray yellow light that was just bright enough for Cyd to make out its eyes, which were staring directly into hers. It gave Cyd a knowing wink and a wry grin, before disappearing completely into the blackness.

Cyd gasped as she was nudged awake.

"Jett again?" Maria asked from the edge of her cot.

"Yeah," Cyd mumbled, wiping the sleep from her bloodshot eyes, "I swear, Mar, every single god-forsaken night I see him again and again, dying on that awful planet... but, you know, something was different about it this time, though."

"Yeah? What?"

"This time, just as he was about to die, a portal-y thing opened up behind him. A being, a specter, came through it and grabbed Jett and Nukii. It looked right at me and smirked. Then they were gone..."

"You should talk to Brother Ziyad," Maria suggested, "you know he was a psychologist before joining the monastery. I read somewhere that when there's a meaningful change in a recurring dream, it means your subconscious mind is trying to tell you something."

"That maybe true for a normal person," Cyd lamented, sighing deeply, "you and I both know how weird our brains are."

"I prefer the term, special," Maria laughed, then turned serious, "you aren't the only one suffering from recurring nightmares, you know."

"I know, Mar, Jett was my best friend, but both of your parents? I couldn't even begin to imagine what that must have been like for you. When I thought I lost my dad forever, I was devastated, but eventually I got him back..."

"The monks taught me how to live with my past," Maria looked down solemnly, "they're the reason I'm alive today. They can help you, too."

"Wow are our lives messed up," Cyd chuckled.

"Yeah," Maria smiled, "Hey, you know what might help you with your nightmares?"

"What?"

"The monks have what they call 'spirit tea'. It's supposed to *calm your soul* and help you sleep better. Brother Arahant mentioned earlier that he was preparing some for a meditation tomorrow morning."

"Well then," Cyd said mischievously, "let's go get some before it's all gone."

"Or we've both lost our minds."

"Whichever comes first."

The two crept to the door of their room and peeked out into the dim hallway. They nodded to each other and tiptoed down the long passage, keeping as quiet as they possibly could given the creaky floorboards and incessant echo. Once they reached the kitchen, Cyd rummaged through the cupboards while Maria inspected a collection of teapots.

"Psst, Mar," Cyd whispered, "I think I found something."

Maria tiptoed over to Cyd who held up a vial marked *enlightenment.*

"It's not what we came here for, but who couldn't use a little enlightenment? I propose a toast," Cyd coaxed, "to our screwed-up minds. May this potion unscrew them!"

"That's not the tea Brother Arahant was making. Are you sure it's okay?"

"I can't promise it'll be okay, but I suspect it'll be enlightening," Cyd smirked.

"To our screwed-up minds," Maria echoed.

In turn, they each took a small sip.

"It's not so ba..." Maria began to say when she fell to her knees, cradling her head in both hands.

"Mar..." Cyd called out, before herself collapsing to the floor.

Maria gasped as vivid images and emotions flooded her mind. A girl in a remote cabin with her parents. Loss. A dark tunnel. Endless frostbitten winter forests. Loneliness. An abandoned cabin on a frozen misty lake. A shaggy red monster holding out it's hand.

Cyd's mind was overwhelmed with images of her father's abduction, Jett standing on a precipice next to a tall man whose black cloak billowed in the wind, the epic battles of Alipour's purple jungles, the all-consuming blood mist, Jack in a hockey rink...

Chapter 4
Fold Takes Notice

The console buzzed incessantly. On a holographic map of the Solaris system, Le-Wa could clearly distinguish a very large cigar shaped craft bound for Solaris 3.

"Our sensors in the Solaris system have picked up an unknown spacecraft."

A hologram of Dr. VaaCaam-a appeared in the center of the room, "Le-Wa, Chi-Col, I understand that you are observing the same phenomenon in the Solaris system that we are. The High Council believes that this vessel may contain the fugitive Hazbog and, possibly, Jett Javelin. If it is Hazbog, his intentions are likely hostile to both the inhabitants of Solaris 3 and to The Fold. We have confirmed that Hazbog is in possession of Fold technologies that could impede our ability to inhibit him."

"The Eelshakian is still far enough from Solaris 3 that we could target his ship with a type-5 neutralization beam without any collateral impact on the planet itself. This will allow us to stop Hazbog's progress and to apprehend both him and the Allpourans. However, our window for action is rapidly closing."

"Very well," Dr. VaaCaam-a approved, "it is permitted."

Le-Wa nodded and turned from VaaCaam-a's hologram. A projection appeared in front of him. It displayed a mesh of Fold satellites and outposts arranged meticulously in a double helix formation across the Solaris system. The image zoomed in on a single strand and then a small grouping of satellites surrounding the mysterious craft. Chi-Col engaged a neutralization net around it.

But no sooner did the neutralization net light up than did every Aaptuuan monitoring device, satellite, and node go offline simultaneously. The Aaptuuan network, for the first time since it was installed in this system millennia ago, was completely offline.

"This is highly unexpected," Le-Wa opined.

"Attempting to bring systems back online..." Chi-Col scrambled.

"Le-Wa, we've detected a large network outage, please apprise us of the situation," Dr. VaaCaam-a insisted.

"It appears that all nodes in the Solaris system, including those on Solaris 9, have become simultaneously unresponsive."

"Throughout our long history, we have never experienced a total systems failure. This was intentional. I fear the Eelshakian has become quite dangerous."

"You believe that the Eelshakian possesses technology sophisticated enough to counter our own?"

"For now, we must assume so, and that he is prepared to use it to destroy Solaris 3."

"How do you wish us to proceed?" Le-Wa asked.

"Go to Solaris 9 and take stock of the colony there. We are dispatching additional resources. They will rendezvous with you at the solar system's edge. Deploy communications nodes along the way so that we may establish a redundant network in the event of a neutralization anomaly."

VaaCaam-a's hologram disappeared.

Le-Wa sighed, "He's locking us out of the system so he can catch the tinker."

Chapter 5
Lanedaar Vue

Tii-Eldii peered out over Lanedaar's vast, dusty red desert. It was as he remembered it, every rock, cliff, ridge, exactly the same as the day he left it behind. He reminisced of his old friend Craabic and wondered if the giant crab still kept guard over the cave where he hid his precious ark for nearly a century. He simultaneously scanned the skies for gull snakes and the horizon for the unmistakable crimson dusk storm of a charlatone swarm.

Tii-Eldii caught a swiftly moving figure out of the corner of his eye. It was bounding through the desert, taking one large leap after another. Tii-Eldii set off after the figure, gliding over the planet's sandy surface as he went. Soon, Tii-Eldii overtook the mysterious figure.

The being stopped and its long black cloak billowed in the wind.

"Greetings stranger, I do not ever recall observing a species such as yours on Lanedaar."

The figure remained silent.

"Do you require shelter? My cave is nearby," Tii-Eldii offered, hoping to coax a response from the mysterious wanderer.

But the figure was unresponsive. Soon it continued onward at a slow, tedious pace, showing no sign that it had heard the Boonan's inquiries or even noticed Tii-Eldii's presence.

"Hello," Tii-Eldii became agitated, "I am trying to help you and you will not even acknowledge me! If it is your desire to be eaten by a gull snake or starve out here then let it be so! I choose to go where it is safe, and I would strongly advise you to do the same." Tii-Eldii barked before marching off toward his cave.

There was no response.

Not willing to be so blatantly ignored, Tii-Eldii stormed back and blocked the figure's path, causing it to look up at him.

Tii-Eldii gasped, "Jett?!"

Jett stared up at him from under the cloak's hood, a forlorn look on his face, "What's a jett?"

Tii-Eldii gasped and his eyes shot open. He jumped out of bed and darted nervously to the window.

"Is everything okay, Tii-Eldii?" Ekiwoo asked groggily, cuddling up to him.

"It's just..." Tii-Eldii started, "It's nothing."

"Tii-Eldii? What this? How many times have I told you to wash your feet before bed? Look at this mess!" Ekiwoo scolded.

Confused, Tii-Eldii looked down at his feet. They were covered in red dust. He looked around. Two sets of red footprints lined the floor. One ended at the side of his bed. The other, a much smaller Solarian set, disappeared into the wall adjacent to where he had been sleeping.

Chapter 6
The Death of the Man on the Moon

"They just stopped responding?" President Montoya demanded, "That's unusual. Are you sure we don't have a systems failure?"

"Sir, we've run every conceivable system diagnostic and the problem doesn't appear to be on our end. All systems check out."

"Well, Mr. Benson, we need to reestablish communication with The Fold, they're expected to arrive on the White House lawn at 14:46, that's 22 minutes from now."

"Yes sir, we will continue running tests until we find something."

"See that you find something soon."

"Yes, sir!"

Montoya's wrist buzzed. He glanced down at his watch. Its screen flashed orange with the code "D2".

"Gentlemen, we are at DEFCON 2," he said.

"Yes, Mr. President, the Pentagon has been informed by NASA that a large spacecraft is passing the moon and its current trajectory will place it above the Mid-Atlantic region of the United States in approximately 22 minutes. All available military aircraft are scrambling, but, if I may say, sir, there are hardly any left in service or pilots to fly the ones we do have."

"Why are we at Defcon 2 if it's the Aaptuuan ship we've been expecting? Why in God's name would we stage a military response? Are we trying to get ourselves neutralized?"

"Mr. President, we've been hailing the spacecraft on all known Fold frequencies, but it isn't responding. We have reason to believe that this may not be a Fold craft, but of unknown alien origin."

"Why would you think that?"

"The ship's design. It resembles some known Aaptuuan craft, but there is one major difference?"

"And what is that, Ms. Setzler?"

"This ship is hostile."

"And how do you know that?"

"Mr. President, the ship in question has vaporized a large portion of our moon."

President Montoya cocked his head, dumbfounded, "Excuse me?"

General Tsao chimed in, "Mr. President, we have received satellite imagery showing the alien craft firing beams of light at the moon. The resulting blasts have removed a piece of the moon's surface roughly the size of Texas. The

Joint Chiefs recommend an immediate full-scale response to this hostile action."

"They just blasted off a Texas sized chunk of the goddamn moon! What do you possibly think a couple of jet fighters are gonna do to stop it? How do we know this thing won't blast off a Texas-sized piece of Texas next? Anyone have another idea?"

General Setzler offered, "We had several advanced laser-based weapon systems in development prior to The Fold's arrival. We could try one of those."

"Let me repeat myself," Montoya said, "they blew off a chunk of the goddamn moon," Montoya shook his head sadly, "General Tsao, have the Pentagon find a way to communicate with whoever or whatever is aboard that vessel. Once they do, patch me in. Have we had any luck raising The Fold on any of the subspace frequencies?"

"Not yet, Mr. President. Every signal we send out is being reflected right back at us. It's like there's a solid wall around the planet and we're stuck in an echo chamber."

"So, in other words, what you're telling me is that this thing is blocking our communication with The Fold?"

"Unfortunately, yes, that appears to be the case."

"Mr. President! We're receiving an inbound communication from the vessel!"

"Put it through."

"Coming through on the monitor now."

The Oval Office's wall monitor flashed to life. On the screen appeared the face of the most hideous creature anyone present had ever set eyes on. Its face was painted with an expression of pure malice. Montoya straightened himself and set his own face with a look of unwavering determination.

"Greetings, Solarians," the creature smirked, "it appears you are curious about my incursion, so you have your audience. I grant you permission to speak."

"Who are you?" The President demanded.

"Were you expecting someone else?" The creature snortled, "I am Hazbog. I would ask who you are, but to be honest, I don't care. As for why I am here, I am collecting something that belongs to me and you are going to help me acquire it."

"What do you mean by that?"

"It is quite simple, really. Out of the kindness of my heart, I am willing to offer you a choice. I will spare your pathetic little planet or I will ravage it in a hell and fury the likes of which you have never known. Hopefully, my demonstration on that pitiful moon of yours emphasizes the urgency with which you need to act. If you should choose for your world to be spared, as you undoubtedly will, I have only one simple demand."

"And what might that be?"

"Your world's savior, Jett Joseph Javelin Jr., the one you all so fondly call 'the Tinker'," Hazbog snarled, "I want him delivered to me by any and every means necessary, and preferably alive."

"Hazbog, if we knew where Jett was, we would comply with your demands, but he's missing and presumed dead."

"Dead? Fools, is that what you think? Your lies betray you! I have personally tracked Jett to this miserable planet, so I know he is here. You have three days to turn him over to me. And if you think The Fold is coming to your rescue, you are sadly mistaken. There is no one coming. The Fold has abandoned you," Hazbog scoffed and the screen became dark.

President Montoya turned to the room and said, "You heard that thing. Start with the Javelin family."

Chapter 7
What the Puck?

"C'mon guys! There are 58 seconds left in the third period and we're one goal away from winning the championship. Williams and Light, I need you both on the center sweep breakout," Jack directed.

"Hey, Javelin, the timeout's almost over. Get back out on the ice," Coach Dubois barked.

"Yes, coach."

"Boys, make it count!"

Jack and his teammates skated out to center ice. He would need to win this face off and get the puck to Williams to set the play in motion. He squared up against his opponent and the puck dropped.

"1-1 game. Sudden death overtime. State championship on the line. Javelin and Lebowski to face off. Javelin gets it off. He's able to get it to Williams," the announcer commentated, "Williams carefully plays it away to Light. Both teams are really giving it their all here tonight. Light snaps it back to Javelin. Javelin is checked by Lebowski. Light scrambles for it and advances it to Williams. Williams shoots, Chen saves on the one-handed stick play and a second one. Rattled on around now and Javelin has it again back out in the center zone. Javelin to Williams. Williams walking it in... He scores! Hey, hey, what do you say? Williams scores! The Bulldogs win!"

Jack, smiling and arms raised high, looked up into the stands where his parents normally sat, but their seats were empty. He scanned the arena. Four men in black suits surrounded his parents at the main exit. One of them spoke firmly to his father, but the roar of the cheering crowd made their conversation impossible to hear. His mother desperately searched the arena with her eyes, but Jack had been swept up in a celebratory sea of teammates and fans, and she couldn't find him, but despite the flailing arms and jumping bodies, it didn't take long for one of the men in black to spot him. The man locked his gaze with Jack's and, without breaking eye contact, proceeded to mutter something into his collar. Then he and two other men shoved their way through the crowd, directly toward him.

"Run!" a voice in Jack's mind commanded, "Run! Now!"

The three men were joined by several more. Some made their way onto the ice while the rest raced through the stands to cut him off. Jack broke free from his team and raced to the gate at the opposite end of the rink. He slammed into the glass, and forcing the gate open, he quickly pried off his skates and sprinted, barefoot, down the maintenance hallway to where the Zamboni was stored.

"Hey, kid, what are you doing in here? Shouldn't you be celebrating with your team?" Zamboni Jim asked him from atop the giant ice cleaning machine.

"Hey, Zamboni Jim. I would be celebrating, but I got a bit of a problem. Can you do me a big favor?"

"Of course, kid. What do you need?"

"There are some men looking for me. I need you to tell them you haven't seen me."

"Sure, but who are they?"

"You haven't seen me, okay?" Jack stressed as he bolted out the open maintenance door, into the dark parking lot, and straight into Abcde.

"Right on time. Let's go," the girl behind her ordered.

"Cyd, what are you doing here?"

"No time, we'll talk later. C'mon! Hurry!"

Cyd and the girl led Jack into the back of a delivery van parked just outside the facility's large metal rollup door.

"Stay down, Jack," Cyd whispered, "hide under these bags. If those men catch you, it's all over. Stay out of sight. We'll let you know when it's safe to come out."

Jack crawled under the pile of empty beige laundry sacks, but his hiding place had already been discovered.

"Hey, you, in the van! Stop right there!"

"Cyd, punch it!"

Abcde slammed the gas pedal to the floor, and the tires squealed. The van lurched forward and Jack was thrown hard against the back doors.

"Hey! Take it easy... You have some fragile cargo back here," Jack mumbled under his breath.

"Cyd turn right here," the girl ordered.

Jack carefully crawled to the front of the van where he grabbed onto the backs of the driver and passenger seats to steady himself.

He stuck his head in between the two girls and said, "Hey, unlicensed driver and girl I don't know, may I ask what the hell is going on? Who are you and who are those guys?"

"Hi, Jack, I'm Maria. Cyd and I just saved your life."

"Again," Cyd smiled, "you're welcome."

"Do you always have to bring up Alipour?"

"It's becoming a pattern with you, this whole saving your life thing. Just sayin'," Cyd teased.

"You two can catch up later," Maria pointed out the windshield, "they're about to cut us off. Step on it!"

A black suv rumbled up alongside them. A man leaning out the window shouted, "Pull over! By order of President Montoya, pull over now!"

"I think not," Maria replied as she swung her arm in a strong upward motion at the vehicle.

The SUV veered off the road and into a ravine where it lodged itself on a low rock wall.

"Holy crap! How did she do that?"

"Did I mention, my friend's a Jedi?" Cyd remarked.

"No, that might've slipped through the cracks during our intense little introduction, sort of like the whole reason you're here. Why are you here, exactly?"

"Well..." Cyd paused a moment, "Remember Hazbog?"

Chapter 8
To Rob & Pillage

"And that, fellow friends of humanity, is what we've learned of Fold vulnerabilities and possible offensive countermeasures. Mr. Chairman, I yield the floor."

The tall man stepped down from the podium and took his seat in the front row of the large subterranean auditorium. The projected image on the screen changed to an Iron Cross.

"Thank you, General Sutter, for making such a compelling presentation. I am convinced by the evidence presented here today and other recent developments, that these unwelcome, uninvited aliens can be kept off our planet. How, you may ask? In addition to General Sutter's excellent revelations, I've invited an anti-Fold patriot and staunch ally of Solaris 3 to enlighten us. People of The Iron, I give you Hazbog of Eelshak, a hero who was held prisoner by The Fold in the dark dungeons of Tower 100, for nearly 3,500 years!"

The claps and cheers fizzled as an electric charge caused every hair in the room to stand on end. The podium microphone squealed. The lights flickered and flashed. A loud pop and flash of light at the back of the giant hall caused the crowd to spin around.

Hazbog appeared grinning devilishly as he returned the crowd's dumbfounded stares. Electricity coursed up and down his body. His eyes swept the room in a way that communicated to all that he was in charge and demanded their respect.

"Chairman Alddon, people of Earth, it is truly a great honor to be greeted by so many good, honest people who share my views of the crooked Fold and their boldfaced lies."

The crowd rose to its feet in a standing ovation.

"The Fold has stolen so much from us all. My own story is a very sad one. The corrupt Fold ravaged my solar system, leaving nothing, not a single atom, in their disastrous wake. I, standing in solidarity with you here today, am all that is left of a once prosperous and peaceful interplanetary civilization. To you, here on Earth, The Fold appears strong, invincible, but let me tell you, people of Earth, The Fold is failing in nearly every corner of The Galaxy. Their subjects are weak and uninspired. Their enemies grow strong as The Fold's influence unravels, and their continued incompetence jeopardizes the future of your planet and many others across the millions of systems they have conquered. But we will not stand idly by. We will expel them from this system!"

The crowd roared, "Expel The Fold! Expel The Fold!"

"Their unjustified neutralizations are catastrophic atrocities that have resulted in mass murder and destruction! Their prescribed *utopia* has stripped you of your position and privilege. You, yes you gathered here today, were once revered, seen as the very pinnacle of human progress. You were the envy of this world. Now look at you. You have been robbed of your greatness, the very thing that makes you unique. You have been reduced to pathetic beggars living off The Fold's table scraps. Nothing more than sad little zoological curiosities. There remains no innovation, no reward, no incentive. They have stolen your humanity. Soon your species will wither away like so many millions of others under The Fold's supposed stewardship. It's that or be neutralized for the mere thought of self-determination. What say you?"

"Expel The Fold! Make Earth great again!" a voice shouted from the crowd.

"And that's precisely what we are going to do. Expel The Fold!" Hazbog bellowed, "To hell with them! Let's lock them all up in Tower 100!"

"Expel The Fold! Make Earth great again!" the crowd chanted, "expel The Fold! Make Earth great again!"

Chapter 9
Securing The Tinker

"I don't understand why you've brought us here, Mr. Smith," Evelyn complained, "Why can't you and your goons leave us alone?"

"Like I said, it's extremely urgent we find your son, Jett. It's a matter of global security."

At the mention of Jett's name, Evelyn burst into tears.

"I'm sorry Mrs. Javelin, I didn't mean to…"

"Agent Smith, with all due respect," Jett Senior interjected, "our son Jett vanished three years ago on some godforsaken planet and hasn't been seen or heard from since. As you are well aware, he was pronounced dead soon thereafter. I don't get why the government feels it necessary to continue to reopen old wounds. This detention is inexcusable! If we knew where Jett was, do you think we'd be keeping it a secret, as if that was even possible?"

"And now Jack's missing, too," Evelyn sobbed, "You and your men frightened him off…"

"Mr. and Mrs. Javelin, we have personnel scouring the Bay Area searching for your son. He couldn't have gotten very far, and we expect to locate him soon."

"You think he'll just walk into custody? He probably saw you hauling us off and ran for the hills."

"Security camera footage at the hockey rink shows your son leaving with two teenage girls in an unmarked Ford Transit van we have confirmed is stolen," Agent Smith continued, "That van was found abandoned five miles south of his last known location off of old Mission Road. We've identified of one of his kidnappers as Abcde Queen. The other's identity is yet to be determined."

"Cyd?" Evelyn asked, "isn't she supposed to be in New Mexico? She and Jack haven't spoken in years, I'm pretty sure since Jett's memorial service. Why would she be here?"

"Agent Smith, are you certain about this?" Javelin asked, "Cyd and Jack had a pretty major falling out. Seems unlikely they would choose to reunite, much less in this manner."

"Yes, Mr. Javelin. Facial recognition and finger-prints left on the steering wheel of their deserted van confirm her identity. We are hoping you might know the other female accomplice," Agent Smith said, turning his tablet around to reveal a grainy shot of Maria in the passenger seat of the van.

"I've never seen her before."

"Mrs. Javelin?"

"I don't recognize her. She must be a friend of Cyd's. Why wouldn't your facial recognition software be able to identify this girl? The Fold has a record of everyone."

"We have some possible matches and leads we're following up on, but so far, no confirmations. Do either of you have any idea where they might have taken Jack?"

"We've already been through this. You obviously know more about Jack's whereabouts than we do. The last time we saw him, he was racing across the ice to get away from you and your men. Why are you so concerned with Jack anyway? I thought it was Jett you're looking for," Evelyn snarled.

"We need to find Jack to ensure his safety, Mrs. Javelin."

"What do you mean?"

"We aren't the only ones looking for him."

"Who else? The Fold?"

Agent Smith's wrist buzzed. He pressed his ear and said, "Yes, sir. I understand. Right away, sir."

"Who was that?" Jett Senior asked.

"That was President Montoya."

"What does he want? Is it about our son?" Evelyn demanded.

"Ma'am, there isn't much going on right now that doesn't concern one or both of your sons. President Montoya has ordered me to return to Washington D.C. immediately."

"Agent Smith, if you're looking for Jett, does that mean he's still alive?"

"Mrs. Javelin, I sincerely hope so because the fate of our planet depends on it. Let's go."

"Where are you taking us?"

"The President has requested your presence at The White House. We leave immediately."

Chapter 10
Winchester's Mystery

"If you were going for creepy, you really nailed it," Jack joked uncomfortably.

"The Winchester Mystery House is only creepy if... Watch your step!" Maria called out as Jack turned and crashed face first into the dilapidated wooden stairs, "Mrs. Winchester was really short and suffered from chronically painful arthritis, so she had baby stairs built. Baby steps, Jack," she cautioned, shining her flashlight on the steps in front of him.

"What the hell am I doing here? I should be at the victory party right now. I should be celebrating with my team," Jack grumbled, climbing back to his feet, "stupid narrow steps! How much farther is this 'secret room' of yours, Maria? And remind me why I'm here again. Seriously."

"We're close. We have to get inside this room because it's the only place in the house, or, come to think of it, the entire bay area, where even Aaptuuan scanners can't find us."

"You obviously don't know the Aaptuuans so well, do you? What do you think is so special about that room?"

"Mrs. Winchester made the room entirely out of lead and encased it in several feet of concrete. She believed lead would repel the spirits of millions who perished at the receiving end of a Winchester rifle. It was discovered last year after a portion of the basement wall caved in, lucky for us," Maria explained, "the vault is several feet thick and should block any kind of life scan, human or otherwise," she stopped suddenly, "What do ya know, here we are," Maria announced, shoving open a dirty metal door that groaned as it disappeared into the pitch black chamber, "Cyd, I think this is the longest I've ever seen you go without talking."

"I'm just..." Cyd thought for a second and shivered, "...taking in the scenery. Not a big fan of ghosts."

"Wuss," Jack sneered stepping through the doorway, "I ain't afraid of no ghosts."

"Are afraid of electric eel monsters?" Maria interrupted.

"You mean Hazbog? I'm pretty sure he's dead. Cyd, you were there. You saw it, too. He fell into the blood mist."

"And he took Jett with him," Cyd reflected, "but I don't believe either of them are dead. Maria and I saw Jett. We know he's alive."

"How exactly? Another one of your weird dreams?"

"Hear me out."

"I figured as much."

"Okay, so here's the deal. The monks Maria and I live with have these teas. A few weeks ago, we tried one and we both had the same dream. Same exact dream and Jett warned us about Hazbog. That's why we came for you."

"Hazbog is using the government to find you, and once he has you, Jack, he'll use you to catch Jett. How do you think we knew you were at the ice rink?" Maria asked, pushing the creaky door closed.

"I don't know."

"Because Jett showed us in the dream."

"Just because the two of you dropped acid in a monastery doesn't mean Jett's alive or Hazbog's looking for me. You were trippin' and you've lost your minds!"

"How do you explain the government's sudden interest in you and your parents? Do you think they were there to watch you win the championship?"

"Cyd, look, you and I've been through all of this. Jett's dead. You need to let it go!"

"Maria and I both saw him. Hazbog is here, and if he made it out of the blood mist alive, maybe Jett did too. Remember, there was a quantum disturbance just before they disappeared."

"Here we go again with the conspiracy theories..."

"Then what do you think happened? You were there!"

Jack's jaw stiffened and his eyes narrowed, "I don't know, okay? Neither do the Aaptuuans, and neither do you. All we know for sure is that Jett and Hazbog were in the blood mist way too long to have survived! I watched that stuff turn animals to dust in seconds, and it almost got me! You're fooling yourself if you think either of them survived, and now you've enlisted your friend here to try and convince me that I didn't see what I saw. I'm out of here. You two can stay down here in this moldy basement for the rest of your lives as far as I'm concerned, but I'm going home."

"Going home to who?" Maria asked.

"Excuse me? I'm going home to see my parents who are probably freaking out about where I am and if I'm lucky, they saved me a piece of cake."

"Jack, guaranteed, the agents who chased us at the rink have taken your parents into custody. They're long gone."

"How do you know that? More conspiracies?"

"Jack, you really need to listen to us. You saw the agents. They weren't there to congratulate you on your big win," Maria said.

"You two deserve each other, you're both crazy. I'm done," Jack pulled the door open and stormed out.

"Jack!" Cyd called.

"Let him go," Maria said, "he won't make it very far."

"How do you know that?"

"First of all, he didn't take a flashlight. Secondly, the nearest exit is a fifteen-minute walk in the dark."

Jack tried not to listen to the girls as he worked his way down the dimly lit hallway. Soon their conversation faded entirely as the creaks and shudders of the old mansion drown it out.

He wandered aimlessly for what felt like hours, with every room more confusing and complex than the last. There were doors that opened into walls and stairs that disappeared into ceilings. The entire time, it felt as though he was being watched, and the hair on his arms and the back of his neck stood on end.

"Are you lost, son?"

Jack practically jumped out of his skin. He spun around, his heart in his throat, and was face to face with a tall lanky old man wearing faded denim overalls, holding a dirty mop.

"You okay son? You get separated from your tour group? Son? Are you with me? You look like you seen a ghost."

"Um... yes, sir. My group... I lost them a couple hours ago and I can't find my way out of here."

"Lord almighty boy, last tour group done left here six hours ago. Here, let me help you. Old Mrs. Winchester was a wily one, made this whole place plum confusin'. Fortunately, fer you, you bumped into me. They call me Winchester Willy seein' as I've worked in this here house for over fitty years. I know e'ry nook and cranny. And you are?"

"Um... Lucas... Skywatcher. My friends call me Luke."

"Well okee-dokee then Mr. Skywatcher, just follow ol' Willy, he knows the way."

Willy led Jack down a series of halls and stairs with the confidence of a man who had lived here all his life.

"Okay, Mr. Skywatcher, we almos' there. I'm surprised the tour group ain't come looking fer you. You ain't the first to get lost in here, but yer the first no one seems to miss."

"Yeah, that is strange. I'll have to take it up with management. We're talking serious lawsuit here," Jack said, feeling a little more comfortable.

"While you ain't the first or last to get lost down here, you might be the first to complain about it. Most of the time, it's ghost hunters and adventure seekers I find lost in the dark. Which are you?"

"Neither, just separated from my school field trip, like I said."

"Uh-huh..."

"You don't believe me?"

"That don't matter none, son. Well, we're here. Sure was a pleasure meeting you, Mr. Skywatcher. The exit's just through there," Willy pointed.

"Thanks Willy," Jack said as he opened the door.

"Yer welcome, son, I hope you find what yer lookin' fer."

"See, I told you he wouldn't make it very far," Maria laughed.

"What? Willy? This isn't the exit..." Jack spun around, but there was no sign of the old janitor.

"Who's Willy?" Cyd asked.

"Winchester Willy! He found me wandering in the halls and told me he'd show me the way out! Where the hell did he go?"

"Jack," Maria said seriously, "Who the hell is Winchester Willie?"

Chapter II
All Love Hazbog

"This is Dan Howard reporting live from Washington D.C. where the alien, Hazbog, claims to have liberated Earth from The Fold and promises to usher in a new era of prosperity. Here's an excerpt from the joint press conference Hazbog held earlier today with President Montoya."

"Citizens of Earth, today is a great day of freedom. My army of Boe warriors has unshackled you from The Fold's oppression and deleterious agenda of learned helplessness. Now your planet may now embrace its greatest invention, the quantum swapper, which will allow your people to have access to everything the Universe has to offer: riches beyond imagination, unlimited power, and eternal life," Hazbog bellowed from the podium, "All of this and much more The Fold sought to deny you, to deny you of what is rightfully yours! In exchange for this great gift of freedom I bestow upon you, I simply ask for one thing in return, just a small token of your gratitude   bring me the Tinker."

"Are there any questions?" Montoya reluctantly asked the crowd of reporters.

"Is it true that a large portion of the moon has been obliterated and that Hazbog and his vessel are responsible?"

Hazbog cocked his head and stared directly at the man who had asked the question. With no need for a microphone, he bellowed, "The Fold's base of operation on your moon was preparing to neutralize Earth as I arrived. I had no choice but to eliminate this threat on your behalf. Did you not wonder why they refused to respond to your communications? But here's the good news, less moon means less tidal influence, and during this time of rising oceans on your planet, you can certainly see the benefit in that. You are lucky I don't ask for additional expressions of gratitude in exchange for this second gift. Next question."

"The person you refer to as 'The Tinker' was pronounced dead several years ago and was last seen alive on another world. What makes you believe that he's still alive and here on Earth?"

Hazbog's face turned serious, "I have searched the galaxy for the tinker following a specific pattern of quantum disturbances. Those disturbances have led me here. It has become clear to me that the tinker is working for The Fold and is responsible for triggering the near neutralization of your planet. The one you know as Jett Javelin, is a traitor to your species and his treasonous actions must be atoned. He is a scourge, a blight. Just as I saved you from The Fold, I will save you from the Tinker."

"What of Pluto and its prisoners?"

"Solaris 9 is unharmed. As soon as I have the Tinker in custody, I pledge to transport your prisoners of war home. But if we are to save those unfortunate souls, time is of the essence."

A muffled chatter rose up from the crowd as those present took in the gravity of Hazbog's words.

Montoya stepped up to the mic, "As you all just heard, Hazbog has generously guaranteed the safe passage of those held on Pluto in exchange for Jett Javelin and any information leading to his apprehension."

A reporter shouted from the back of the room, "Life under The Fold was prosperous for everyone. How can we trust this creature? What are his credentials?"

Another asked, "What if we can't or won't turn over Jett Javelin?"

Hazbog brushed Montoya to the side and said, "It is not much I ask. I know he is here. You will bring him to me, and, I may have neglected to mention, I will need you to do this within the next three rotations. Otherwise, I will interpret your inaction to mean you are ungrateful. That is all,"

Hazbog finished, turning from the mic and lumbering backstage.

A cacophony of questions rose up.

"Do you mean three days?"

"President Montoya, can you expand on what he means by 'ungrateful'?

"This press conference is over," Montoya ordered, "We must find the Tinker. Leave no stone unturned."

The image cut back to Dan Howard standing on the sidewalk in front of The White House.

"There you have it. Lots of questions, but not so many answers," Dan Howard reported.

"Dan, has any additional information come out of The White House concerning Jett Javelin?" Barbara asked.

"No, the government has been unusually quiet since reporters were escorted out of the briefing room. We do know that citizens across the globe have taken to the streets searching for the tinker. Social media is abuzz with the hashtags - #tinkerfold, #tinkergate, and #hazbogtruth."

"Dan, do we have any indication who the alien Hazbog is or where he comes from and why he is so interested in Jett Javelin?"

"Well, Barbara, Hazbog has only said that he opposes The Fold and travels the galaxy freeing subjugated planets from their tyranny. We do not know where he hails from or why he is interested in Jett Javelin. Nor do we know what will happen to Earth if we are unable to comply. This reporter is hoping we find a way to find the tinker."

"Thanks, Dan. We'll be checking in with you throughout the search."

"Thanks, Barbara."

"And for you viewers at home: how will you find the tinker? Send your photos and videos to @foxbc and tag #thesearchison. Good luck! The fate of Earth rests on your shoulders. What are you waiting for? Get out there and find the tinker! Godspeed!"

Chapter 12
Winchester Willie

"What do you mean who's Winchester Willy? I was just with him ten seconds ago!" Jack argued, "He's the janitor. He was as real as either of you."

Abcde and Maria looked back at him as though he had lost his mind. Was he imagining things? He was certain Willy was there talking with him *and* Jack could hear the floorboards squeaking beneath his feet as he walked. Ghost feet don't do that.

"I'm not making this up. Look, he told me he would show me the way out. Instead he brought me back here which is the last thing I wanted."

"Stop being so dramatic," Cyd ordered, "you were probably seeing things. This place can play tricks on you."

"Or maybe you guys slipped me some of your crazy monk-shrooms and I'm hallucinating! How about that?"

"No one slipped you anything, Jack. Everyone knows this place is haunted. I doubt it was the Janitor. You probably just saw your first ghost."

"I know what I saw, okay, and it wasn't a ghost. You two are making me crazy. Let's just drop it!"

"Agreed," Cyd and Maria said in unison.

"So now what?" Jack asked with an annoyed tone, "Sit here until another ghost shows up?"

"Well, we need to lay low down here for a while and hopefully the government and Hazbog will move on and look somewhere else," Maria instructed, "then once we get out of here, we need to head north."

"That's great. Hide here, head north," Jack remarked, "and what the hell are we supposed to do while we're down here? We don't have any food or water and I don't suppose either of you brought Monopoly."

Maria took off her backpack and laid it on the floor between them. She opened it up and revealed bottles of water, zip-lock bags of nuts and granola, dozens of meal replacement bars, and an assortment of camping and hiking accessories. Cyd did the same.

"So, no on the board games... Any chance either of you brought a Dr. Pepper?"

Cyd smiled knowingly at Jack. She opened a velcro flap inside her pack and presented a single can of Jett's favorite drink.

"Are you serious?" Jack puzzled, "I was kidding."

"I didn't bring it for you. I brought it for Jett."

"Give me a break! When are you going to give it up already? You know you're just torturing yourself."

"I have to keep hope alive. We never know when he might show up."

"I don't get it, but whatever. I don't want it anyway and neither would Jett. It's warm... Tell me, other than sitting here eating date bars and singing kumbaya before eventually 'heading north', do you actually have a plan?"

"First thing we'll need to do before we leave is disguise you. We brought some stuff to wear," Cyd pulled out a black satin sack and emptied its contents on to the floor. There was a flowery dress, wig, stockings, and makeup kit."

"You're not dressing me up like a drag queen!"

"C'mon Jack, I dressed like a commando," Cyd pointed out, "Look at my hair. Why do you think I cut it so short?"

"Going butch, maybe?"

"Get real."

"Jack, if we don't use a lot of makeup and a wig, facial rec or anyone of a million people out in the streets searching for you will spot you in a second. Game over." Maria pointed out, "If you're not willing to work with us, we may as well turn ourselves in right now."

"Supposing I go along with this half-baked plan of yours, after we play dress up, then what? Head north?" he smirked.

"Tomorrow night, we'll make our way to Santa Cruz. There we'll meet up with a fisherman who will take us north to Eureka. From Eureka we'll head inland to Maple Creek and north again to Fernwood. Once we arrive in Fernwood, I have some friends who will protect us."

"Wow, you've really thought this through. Just so you know, it's a haul from here to Santa Cruz, which is south, by the way. And forget Eureka. And I have no idea where Fernwood is, but I'm pretty sure the government or Hazbog will catch us long before we get to any of those places."

"We'll take the sewer system as far as we can. There's an old entrance at the other end of the basement. Once we exit the sewer, I know a path through the woods that will take us to the coast."

"Let's see if I understand this: the plan is to dress me up like a girl and then take the sewer to the woods to some random boat to more woods where some friends of yours will hide us from the all-seeing eyes of the government."

"I think he's got it," Cyd teased.

"Well, I'm exhausted, if we're gonna stay here for a while, then I'm getting some shut eye," Jack muttered, "guess I'll just curl up in the corner like a homeless person. Thanks for bringing sleeping bags," he remarked sarcastically.

Jack laid down on the cold hard floor. His mind reviewed the events of the day and he hoped desperately that when he woke up, he would be in his own bed, with all of this adventure, including Winchester Willie, being nothing but an unpleasant dream. He eventually fell asleep as the physical exhaustion of the hockey game and the mental exhaustion of Cyd, her friend, and the entire situation overwhelmed him.

Cyd and Maria followed suit, each picking a spot on the floor. Using their backpacks as pillows, they, too, were soon asleep.

Jack dreams featured the championship party after the game. There was a large frosted multi-layered cake with a plastic goalie on top, and his mother handed pieces to everyone. As Jack walked up to get his piece, a man at the front of the line turned around with cake in hand.

"Hey kid, you have any Dr Pepper?"

"Winchester Willie?" Jack gasped and shot up straight as a board. In the one corner of the room where no one had slept was an open can of Dr Pepper laying on its side, a trickle of the brown soda dribbling on the floor.

"Cyd, wake up! Wake up, I said!"

"What is it, Jack?"

"Quiet down Jack, you'll wake the dead!" Maria complained.

"Oh, I think they're already awake."

"Why is that?" Cyd asked incredulously.

"You said the Dr Pepper was for Jett, right?"

"Yeah, why?"

"I think Winchester Willy beat him to the punch," he pointed.

Chapter 13
Reflections

The three of them stared at the empty soda can in disbelief. Because Cyd was sleeping on her backpack, it would have been impossible for someone to have removed the can without disturbing her. Yet, there it was on the floor, empty.

"Jack, tell me you drank the Dr Pepper."

"Nope, I hate warm soda. I'm pretty sure it was Winchester Willy."

"For the last time, there is no Winchester Willy!" Maria snarled.

"Then who the hell brought me back here? I'm pretty sure a figment of my imagination couldn't do that."

"You think it was Jett?" Cyd asked hopefully.

"If Jett is still alive, which is a big if, a huge if, why would he come in here, drink the soda, and bail? Be real. There's no way."

"Well, however that soda got drank, I'm starting to freak out. I say we get out of here and start making our way to Santa Cruz. The sooner we get to Fernwood, the better," Cyd suggested, "Something's not right."

"I'm good with that," Jack agreed, "Let's get me dressed up."

"Was bound to happen sooner or later," Cyd said.

"I'm not so sure about that."

"Let's do this," Maria handed Jack the flower pattern dress, "go ahead and put this on. There's a mirror in the hallway just outside the door."

Jack reluctantly accepted the garments and stepped into the hallway to change while the girls readied his makeup.

Jack slipped the dress on. To his surprise, it was a perfect fit. However, as Jack stepped in front of the dusty old mirror to see how ridiculous he looked, it was not his face in the mirror staring back at him. Instead, wearing the same yellow flower pattern dress, Winchester Willy, with a slight twinkle in his eye, grinned widely back at Jack.

Heart pounding in his chest, Jack opened his mouth to call for help, but regardless of how hard he tried to scream, he was mute. Not a sound came out. Worse, he was frozen. All he could do was stand there and stare at Willie in the mirror.

Willy's expression changed from a smile to a sneer. He reached out from the mirror and grabbed a hold of Jack's shoulders.

"What's taking you so long?" Cyd asked, sticking her head out into the hallway.

Jack opened his eyes. Willy was gone. Jack turned back to his reflection in disbelief.

"Everything, okay?"

"You wouldn't believe me if I told you. Let's get the hell out of here."

"You didn't see Willy again, did you?"

"Forget it," Jack hurried past her to the safety of the lead room.

Cyd walked over to the mirror and looked into it for a moment. Then she looked up and down the hallway once or twice, shrugged, and followed Jack back into the room.

When they returned, Cyd had the makeup ready and they got down to business, but it wasn't easy. Jack's encounter in the hallway caused him to shiver and fidget nervously while Maria attempted to paint his face.

"Stop moving around! You're gonna make me screw up. Stop! I'm gonna poke you in the eye," Maria complained, "Cyd, can you help me here?"

Cyd walked up behind Jack and placed a hand on each side of his head to steady him.

"You're shaking like a leaf," she observed.

She closed her eyes and concentrated so hard that her face puckered up. She felt a strange sensation as she became Jack peering into the mirror. There, an old man in a yellow dress stared lecherously back. Then he lunged out and grabbed her. Cyd recoiled in horror and released Jack's head.

"What's the matter, Cyd?"

"Mar, we need to get the hell out of here."

"I'm doing this as fast as I can. A little help, please."

"No, I mean it. We need to go right now. Jack's telling the truth. Something else is in here with us."

"Did you see him, too?" Jack asked nervously.

"I saw him in the mirror."

"Saw who in the mirror?" Maria asked.

"An evil spirit... in a flower dress..."

"Winchester Willy! I wasn't hallucinating."

"Nope. I saw him. Not good. Gotta go. Now!"

They shared an awkward minute of silence. None of them was sure what to say or do next.

Finally, Maria placed the long blond wig on Jack's head and stepped back, both to admire her work and make a couple of fine adjustments.

"A little more lip gloss here and a tuck there, and Ms. Javelin... you make a pretty ugly girl, but hopefully that'll keep people from looking at you too closely."

"Ha, ha, ha. Can we leave now?"

"After you, my lady," Maria said taking a sweeping bow toward the door.

"It's nice to see chivalry isn't dead," Jack muttered.

They went past the mirror. Jack and Cyd averted their eyes and walked a bit faster than Maria, who paused to look at it quizzically.

"Hurry up, you're the only one who knows the way out of here!" Cyd urged.

"We're going to need to make a slight adjustment to our plan," Maria reflected as she jogged to catch up.

She led them down several dimly lit hallways and up a couple flights of winding stairs until they finally reached the main ballroom. The entire time, Jack kept looking over his shoulder and around every corner, expecting to catch a glimpse of Willy or confront him face to face, but the mysterious ghost was nowhere to be found. Jack breathed a massive sigh of relief when Maria finally opened a door marked Exit and they all walked outside onto the rickety wooden porch.

"Great! Our Uber is already here," Maria announced.

"Uber? I thought we were taking the sewer, not that I'm complaining," Jack said, "When did you call an Uber?"

"Does it matter? Our speedy departure required a change of plan."

"Won't they be able to track us?"

"Nope, stolen phone," Maria grinned, "but we only get one shot with it. I was hoping to save it, but what's done is done," she stopped and said sharply, "Try not to look into the dashcam. Facial rec can see through makeup," she pulled some of the blond hair around Jack's face, "and sit in the rear facing seat. Walk behind me."

They hastily pushed their way through the main gate and onto the decomposed gravel parking lot. The rocks crunched loudly beneath their feet. Maria did her best to shield Jack from the car's cameras. The autonomous car's large side door slid open.

"Is Santa Cruz your destination?" the car asked.

"Yes, please. I'll let you know where to let us out," Maria said.

"Confirmed. Estimated travel time to Santa Cruz is forty-seven minutes in light traffic."

The egg-shaped white car pulled out of the parking lot onto the main road, Jack looked back at the Winchester House. On the front porch stood a smiling Winchester Willy. He raised a can of Dr. Pepper in his right hand in a mock toast.

Chapter 14
The Roadless Traveler

They are beautiful, Hazbog thought to himself as he gazed down from his private quarters in orbit above the Western Hemisphere. A billion lights outlining two continents twinkled below him, casting the dark side of Solaris 3 in a warm glow.

"It's a shame I'll have to snuff them out. Life's unfair," he opined.

A figure materialized in the shadows behind Hazbog and strolled up next to him. The lanky being stood nearly seven feet tall and was dressed as a highly decorated Eelshakian general.

"Always so dramatic. Why does everything with you always have to be so dramatic? It's off-putting."

Hazbog turned his head slightly toward the being and replied, "Is it not true? Once we have the tinker, no one will miss this worthless little backwater. It's the perfect test for our ion cannon. Their moon was just a little tidbit."

"See, that's what I'm talking about. It's tragic that there aren't any more of our kind left to share in all the drama," the Eelshakian smirked, "the greatest empire the galaxy has ever known, snuffed out... we are all that's left of

Eelshak. All that will be left of Solaris 3, is Jett Javelin. Fitting, no?"

"Perhaps."

"The reverse neutralization has thrown The Fold on its heels. Never in their history has their genocidal technology been used against them. I must commend you Hazbog. They are blind to all we do here. You have a deep knowledge of their technology, especially for a janitor," he laughed.

"I was never meant to be a janitor. That mindless assignment was an affront to my abilities. 3,500 years is a long time to learn anything, so I decided to learn everything."

"I agree. It appears The Fold has created a monster to contend with. It was bound to happen. So meddlesome. Now, let's get to the matter at hand. Have you located Mr. Javelin?"

"Most Solarians believe he died on Alipour. We have apprehended his progenitors and they are being interrogated, but his sibling has proven more difficult to capture, and continues to elude us. We believe he is being aided by the one called Abcde and another female who remains unidentified. We expect to take them all into custody very soon. While the sibling may be of little help, his abettors are of great interest."

"Why is that?" the Eelshakian asked.

"The one called Abcde, according to Fold archives has advanced psychic abilities and a strong mental link to Jett Javelin. She was able to locate Jack Javelin and me on Alipour, so I'm certain she knows where Jett is. We have interviewed several Solarians that know her, and they say she has had similar visions recently involving both Jett and Jack Javelin. This explains how she and her unknown accomplice were able to intercept the brother moments before our agents arrived."

"That is an interesting little wrinkle. Does the girl know about us?"

"The entire planet knows of me, but your presence remains hidden. Are you certain Jett is here?"

"Yes, Hazbog, he is. His quantum trail ends here. I am sure of it. Yet somehow the tinker and his friends continue to elude you. It is odd that someone as experienced as you claim to be, an officer of the great Eelshakian navy, would be unable to complete such a small task as finding a few juvenile fugitives. Perhaps, it's time for me to find another more capable partner."

Hazbog growled, "How dare you! I am the commander of this ship and this system. Now that I know the tinker is here, consider our partnership dissolved."

Hazbog lunged at the being, but as he did, every muscle in his body froze, every hair stood on end. Hazbog, teeth clenched, stood still as a statue, with outstretched claw trembling centimeters from the being's neck.

"You're not Eelshakian... What are you?" Hazbog managed to choke out.

"Me? Just a weary traveler," the being grinned devilishly, "but mostly just weary of you. See to it that you find Mr. Javelin and his friends or the next time I suspend you, it'll be in the vacuum of space."

With a slight circular motion of his hand, the being summoned an oval portal behind him. Its blue light swirled in a lazy counterclockwise pattern.

Before he stepped into the energy field he turned and said, "Don't disappoint me, Hazbog."

"Yes, Ripeem," Hazbog hissed through clenched teeth.

And then, with a slight tip of his broad brimmed hat, the Eelshakian General was gone.

Hazbog, no longer frozen, stumbled forward and caught himself on the edge of a table.

"Summon my commanders! Dispatch the first regimen to the surface!"

"Yes, Hazbog," a warm computer voice answered.

"I want every inch of this planet scoured. Leave no stone unturned!"

Hazbog glared at the place where the being had stepped into its portal, "Time to renegotiate our deal, I'm afraid. Whatever you are, it's time you learned your place."

Chapter 15
The Tides Wait for Me

The fog hung low in the forest. Jack peered out from inside a large redwood tree that had been hollowed out by an ancient fire. Icy wind bit into his bones. He rubbed his hands together in a vain attempt to keep warm. His yellow summer dress wasn't helping matters.

"Can I please have my clothes back? This is the kind of dress they ban in private schools," Jack complained gesturing to the goosebumps covering his mid-thigh, "and for good reason. I'm freezing here!"

Cyd shot back, "Stop your bitching. It's the best we could do on such short notice. They don't make a lot of women's clothes for six-foot two hockey players. You're lucky we found anything at all."

"Yeah, real lucky…"

Maria sat quietly and scrutinized a set of old paper maps. She used a red sharpie to plot their journey to Fernwood.

"They still print those things? Would have been much easier if you hadn't tossed a perfectly good phone out the car window."

"Jack, let me remind you that, after your brother, you are the second most wanted fugitive on this planet. Using anything with GPS would put this whole operation at risk," Maria remarked, "from here on out, it's paper maps, compasses, and navigation by the stars."

"Okay, Galileo, just don't get us lost out here. I don't want to become Bigfoot food."

"You needn't worry about that. They're vegetarian."

"And how do you know this?"

"I just do."

"Really..."

"Jack, you need to lighten up. Okay, then. Let's review. We'll hike down this ridge," Maria pointed to one of her maps, "and cross the highway. We'll make our way down to this inlet, here. The locals tend to stash their kayaks at the base of the cliff. We will each commandeer a kayak and paddle out this reef. At approximately 3pm, we will rendezvous with a twenty-nine-foot boat piloted by Brother Duc. He will take us up the coast to Eureka."

"And you're sure he'll be there," Cyd said.

"You of all people should know he'll be there."

"You both assume there will be a pile of kayaks just sitting in the sand waiting to be stolen and that no one will be around or care. This plan seems fundamentally flawed if you ask me," Jack shivered, "And who's Brother Duck guy? Was Captain Hook busy?"

"Do you want to take this one?" Maria asked Cyd.

"Sure. Brother Duc is... one of the more eccentric Buddhist monks in the monastery."

"Is he that one that hands out psychedelic drugs to underage girls?"

"No one gave those to us, we stole them from the kitchen," Cyd interjected.

"Lovely. They keep the drugs in the kitchen."

"C'mon you two," Maria interrupted, "Let's just say he's not what you would expect from a Buddhist monk. He escaped from Vietnam in a skiff when he was fifteen years old and sailed across the Pacific Ocean by himself. He made landfall near Santa Barbara several months later having survived on nothing but sea gulls, turtles, and rainwater. He is more than qualified to take us up the California coast."

"Let's hope he's updated the menu for this trip," Jack remarked.

The three packed up camp and made their way to the ridge trail. Jack's icy legs began to burn and itch as he huffed his way up the craggy path. He was grateful that at least the girls had let him keep his sneakers. Hiking through these dense woods in heels would've proven impossible.

Once they reached the ridgeline, the rolling hills spilled down into the ocean. A single lighthouse perched on a promontory below them.

"That's it!" Maria called, "That lighthouse is just south of the inlet. C'mon!"

They quickly wound their way down the narrow dirt trail while the waste high grass and mustard hissed and swayed in the erratic wind. A small herd of mule deer grazed in a thicket just before the next rise. They displayed little fear as the three hikers approached and continued munching away as if there weren't a human for a thousand miles.

When they reached the highway, they stopped to rest and have a drink of water. Maria pulled out one of her wrinkled paper maps and unfolded it on the ground in front of them.

"There's a drainage pipe that runs under the highway about a half mile north of here. We'll have to double back a bit on the other side, but at least none of the traffic cameras will spot us."

"Let's go," Cyd started to say when a California Highway Patrol SUV pulled over to the side of the road just above where they hid in the underbrush.

"Get down!" Maria yanked both their shoulders.

"All units be on the lookout for three adolescents - two females and one male, believed to be in the vicinity. They are fugitives and may be armed and dangerous. They were last seen by an autonomous ride share vehicle's onboard facial rec camera exiting near Moore Creek Preserve and heading west into the forest."

Jack and Cyd both shot Maria a look. Maria looked down and away.

"If you encounter these fugitives, do not apprehend. Maintain your distance and call for backup. They are not to be harmed in any way by direct order of The President of the United States."

As quickly as it arrived, the patrol car sped off.

"If the local cops think we're in the area, it's probably crawling with feds."

Maria looked up and down the highway. There were no cars or cameras visible in either direction.

"Coast is clear. Let's run for it!" she yelled as she charged up the slope and across the highway.

"She's insane! She can't even stick to her own plan!" Jack shouted leaping up with Cyd following close behind.

They arrived on the other side of the highway and barreled down the embankment into the fragrant sage and scrub brush where they dropped out of sight.

"Are you out of you mind?" Cyd scolded, "You could have gotten yourself killed or all three of us captured."

"Oh, please."

"She flipped a Chevy Tahoe at the hockey rink," Jack said.

"That's great. And what do you think her car flipping antics will do for us here?"

"We made it here and that's all that matters. Plus, we saved a bunch of time by not going through the tunnel. Let's head down to the beach and pick out some kayaks."

They reached the sand in a few short minutes and, just as Maria had predicted, dozens of kayaks were stacked against the base of a rounded sandstone cliff. She ran over to the closest stack and attempted to pull one of the top, but they were all locked together with a long metal cable.

"Fundamentally flawed I said..."

"Jack, you underestimate me," Maria smiled as she produced a set of bolt cutters from her backpack and cut the cable, "go ahead and grab one. We need to get out to the reef asap."

They each selected and dragged a kayak down to the deserted waterline and paddled out past the break. When they reached the reef, Maria checked her watch. It was 2:45pm. She scanned the horizon and was able to make out the silhouette of a boat rapidly approaching them.

Maria pointed, "That's Brother Duc."

"And hopefully not the Coast Guard," Jack added.

At 3:00pm sharp, a sailboat slowly pulled alongside Maria's kayak. A man dressed in a dark blue overcoat and baseball cap came to the port side.

He offered Maria his hand, "Come on, we must hurry. There were agents and drones all over the harbor."

One after another, the man pulled them all aboard. Jack looked back at the shoreline. As the late afternoon fog began to settle in, he watched a crowd gathering near the kayaks and pointing out to the reef.

"I think the locals may be on to us," he said.

Brother Duc smiled, "They won't be for long. We're about to vanish into the mist. In any case, I brought the big guns," he gestured to two large outboard motors.

The twin engines roared, and the boat surged forward. The thrust sent all three kayaks flipping and rolling in the boat's wake. Brother Duc steered boat turned out to sea.

"This fog is a real lifesaver," Maria said.

"Sometimes it's better to be lucky than to be good," Brother Duc responded.

Chapter 16
Boe Unleashed

President Montoya glared at his staff in frustration, "What do you mean you can't find them. We have facial rec video from an autonomous Uber along with a geo tagged location where they were dropped off! They're kids on foot in the woods. Stop telling me you can't find them!"

"Sir, we have nearly a thousand marines scouring the woods around Santa Cruz. Air units have been deployed and drones are swarming the area. I have no doubt we will find them."

"You keep telling me that, but you keep coming up empty."

"Have you considered that they may no longer be in Santa Cruz?" Hazbog's gravelly voice asked as he materialized by the window overlooking the Rose Garden. His unexpected appearance riled the room.

"With respect, Hazbog, we have checkpoints on every road and patrols on every footpath in that sector. There is no way they could have escaped by foot or vehicle," answered General Tsao, "we will have them in custody shortly."

"No, you won't," Hazbog snarled, "because they are no longer in your so-called Santa Cruz! I grow weary of the uniquely low IQ that powers the Solarian brain. No matter, due to gross incompetence, I am forced to relieve General Tsao of his responsibilities," Hazbog extended his arm and rested it on General Tsao's shoulder, "let this be a lesson for the rest of you," he seethed, jolting the general's body with a powerful flash of electricity.

General Tsao shook erratically and dropped to the ground, twitching like a chicken whose head had been cut off until his body dissolved into ash. The smell of charred human flesh hung heavily in the air.

"I'm afraid I overcooked General Tsao. Ha! Ha! Ha! You," Hazbog pointed to a timid looking man in round spectacles, "where do you think these criminals might have gone?"

The man swallowed hard, choking on his words, "I guess they... they... could have gone out to sea?"

Hazbog smirked and bent over to pick up the general's ash filled hat. He approached the cowering man and placed the steaming hat on his head. Ash poured down onto the man's face, and he choked uncomfortably.

"Congratulations, you have just been promoted. You very well may be the most intelligent creature in this dump. So, let me ask you, if they left by sea, then they must be in a…?"

"B…b…b…boat? S…s…sir?"

"That is correct. They are in a boat. That boat is heading north out in the open sea at this very moment, and you idiots are looking in the woods!"

A visibly perturbed President Montoya pushed his way across the room to Hazbog.

"You just reduced my best general to ash in my office in front of my staff! Who the hell do you think you are?!"

Hazbog calmly turned to Montoya. He towered over The President, but Montoya stood firm, not yielding a millimeter.

"My, my, my aren't we testy? Don't worry, I have a cure for that," Hazbog declared lifting Montoya by his shirt. The President's feet dangled in the air, "Have something to say do you? Well we will see about that," Hazbog continued, but before he could do whatever it was he was planning, Montoya unexpectedly fell to the ground with a thud.

Hazbog, perplexed, stared at his arm in horror, turning it round and round in confusion. Montoya frantically scooted back, gasping for air, until he was pressed against his desk. He pulled himself up slowly, and although he was clearly shaken, he confronted Hazbog once again.

"What's the matter, Hazbog?"

Hazbog shook his head and growled angrily, "I do not know to what you are referring, Solarian. You should appreciate my mercy and not press your luck. Due to your continued incompetence, I have dispatched a contingent of my finest warriors to assist in locating these children. Do not test me, Montoya, the fate of your precious little planet hangs in the balance. If you do not locate Jack or Jett Javelin before my warriors do, my little bespectacled friend here will be promoted to your position. Ashes to ashes and dust to dust," Hazbog cackled as he slowly vanished.

Montoya took a moment to collect himself. He stared down at the pile of ashes that was once his finest general, confidant, and friend. He turned to one of the soldiers in attendance, "Please collect the general's remains. He deserves to be buried with full military honors."

"Right away, sir!"

Montoya took a moment of silence before continuing, "Ladies and gentlemen, you all heard that maniac. I want every resource we have off the coast of California immediately! Every boat, every plane, every drone, every helicopter, everything! Now!"

Aloft in orbit, Hazbog examined his arm in disbelief, as it phased in and out of existence.
"What is happening to me..."

Chapter 17
The Tormentors

Wailing sirens blared across Boona. Young and old scurried underground, seeking shelter from the looming extraterrestrial threat that lurked just above the planet.

"Warning, warning, this is not a drill. Tormentor ship detected entering upper stratosphere over the continent of Javeland. All citizens are urged to report to their assigned bunkers. Warning, warning, this is not a drill. All citizens please report to your assigned bunker. Tormentor vessel inbound. Repeat, Tormentor vessel inbound over Javeland. Clear all public thoroughfares immediately. Warning, warning. This is not a test."

Tii-Eldii elbowed his way through the panicking crowd, surprised that the Aaptuuans had waited so long to make an appearance. After Jett's departure to Earth, there were a few months when the entire planet held its collective breath waiting for some kind of retribution, but The Fold took no action. Much to their surprise, Boona's power remained on and after a few short years, the once dark civilization reestablished itself as a center of art, philosophy, and technology. Few believed that the Tormentors would return so long as the planet abided by The Ten Laws of Civilized Living.

There were a few in positions of power who felt that the population should, nonetheless, be prepared for, what they believed, was the inevitable return of The Fold and its agents. To avoid the death and devastation of another potential neutralization, massive public works projects were undertaken to construct vast underground bunkers. These were subsequently outfitted with massive amounts of food, water, clothing, tools, and anything else deemed necessary in a post neutralization world.

With over a century of experience in the matters of neutralization, the Boonans cleverly constructed means of production that could be reliably operated without any electricity at all. These employed sophisticated mechanical systems driven by hydro, steam, or animal power that could be quickly brought online in the event the planet's power was suddenly cutoff. They successfully built a new world that could operate nearly as efficiently without electricity as with it. With The Fold's arrival imminent, all of their careful planning was about to be put to the test.

Tii-Eldii's collar buzzed.

"Where are you?" Ekiwoo pleaded, "We are all here in the shelter waiting for you."

Tii-Eldii looked up into the sky and watched as an Aaptuuan craft descending through the thick gray morning clouds.

He responded, "I can see them. One of their ships is directly above me."

"What are you doing, Tii-Eldii? Get down here now!" she ordered, "It's not safe up there!"

"I will..." Tii-Eldii began to say when the craft made a sudden right-angled maneuver in his direction, "they are coming directly towards me..."

"Get out of there!"

Tii-Eldii's tone shifted, "If they come to me, I will see what they want."

"Tii-Eldii!" Ekiwoo cried, but he powered his comm-link off.

The rapidly approaching spacecraft came to a sudden stop just fifteen meters above his head. A hatch opened and a warm beam of light engulfed the Boonan scientist. It drew him up and into the craft. Tii-Eldii was brought into a white room with no doors, windows, or defining features of any kind. He stood there waiting nervously for a few moments before a door materialized in a wall opposite him and two Aaptuuans entered.

"Greetings, Tii-Eldii," one of them telepathed, "you may remember us from your cave on Lanedaar 3 where my associate here was nearly eaten by your friend Craabic. I believe you are the one who *borrowed* our ship. We have not been formally introduced. I am Chi-Col and this is Le-Wa."

Tii-Eldii swallowed hard, "If you have come for your ship, it is currently on display at the The Museum of The Great Darkness. You will find that it is more or less inoperable now that its energy source has been depleted. I am sure you have a means of repairing this deficiency. I can take you there."

"We have not come for our ship. Let your people keep it as a reminder of that unfortunate chapter in your planet's history. We are here for another reason. Tii-Eldii, we have come for you. We require your help."

"You require my help? How can I possibly help you?"

"An escaped fugitive named Hazbog has successfully escaped our planet and is holding Solaris 3 hostage as he aggressively seeks the whereabouts of Jett Javelin. We suspect he is interested in the boy's quantum technology since he is in possession of the only working example."

"I am confused. Why can you not stop this fugitive? What can I possibly offer you?"

"Hazbog has co-opted Fold technology for his bellicose purposes and we know little of the ways of war. Beyond that, we are forbidden from waging such. We require your species' strength and agility to battle Hazbog and his army of Alipouran warriors on Solaris 3."

"Why doesn't The Fold simply neutralize Hazbog and his army? This seems to be your tactic of choice."

"Hazbog has managed to create a shield around Solaris 3 by reversing our neutralization mesh. Any attempt to reach the planet will result in the total and utter neutralization our fleet."

"Someone has finally outsmarted you and with your own weapon, too. How does it feel?"

"It is very unpleasant, but with your help, the feeling will be short-lived. While in almost any other circumstance we would let Hazbog and the Boe have their way with Solaris 3, you can agree that the Tinker is a special consideration."

"Indeed. You will find that all Boonans feel deeply indebted to Jett because he freed us from the evil you set upon our people. Yet after these atrocities, The Fold has the audacity to ask Boona for help? This will not be well received."

"We understand how your people, and particularly you, feel towards Jett Javelin. This is precisely why we have come. We cannot take back The Fold's previous mandates nor would we if we could, but we ask you to consider this: since Jett returned you to Fabboett, The Fold has left your power restored and granted your planet a rare reprieve. This does not mean we expect you to forgive or forget what was done. We prefer that you and your people always remember The Darkness, as you call it, as a painful, but necessary lesson that has hastened your societal evolution. No, we do not seek forgiveness, we simply seek your assistance to help us rescue the being who saved your people."

"From The Fold!"

"Most assuredly."

"I find this most puzzling," Tii-Eldii muttered, "as we discuss this request of yours, the entire Boonan civilization has gone underground in anticipation of a second neutralization. While I personally will do whatever you ask with regards to Jett, I believe that convincing my brethren to follow suit will prove difficult. How can we trust you?"

"Your people will not trust us, but they will trust you, and they will want to save Jett. Time is running out. If we do not act quickly, there is no telling what Hazbog will do to the Tinker or his planet. Will you help us?"

As Tii-Eldii considered their plea and how he might sell it to the Boonan populace, he remembered his dream.

"What's a jett?" Le-Wa repeated Tii-Eldii's thoughts.

"How do you know about that?"

"Le-Wa and I have recently experienced similar dreams," Chi-Col responded, "we believe Jett is attempting to communicate with a select few from the confines of a parallel universe where he is trapped."

"Trapped?" Tii-Eldii asked.

"One of the side effects of Quantum Swapping, I am afraid."

"Side effects?"

"Jett is caught between two universes. Existing in multiple dimensions simultaneously is a side effect of quantum sickness."

"Jett's ill?"

"Tii-Eldii, there is much to discuss, but first you must give us your commitment. Will you help Jett?"

"Yes..."

Chapter 18
Not to be Trusted

The immense body of the Boonan planetary government stood gathered in the massive chamber before him. Once Tii-Eldii agreed to help The Fold enlist Boona's help, it was decided that it would be best if the Aaptuuans waited in orbit for their answer. Their continued presence on the planet's surface was a source of great distress for the populace. Immediately following their withdrawal, Tii-Eldii was summoned to the Parliamentary complex where he was deposed to answer charges concerning his involvement with The Tormentors.

"Let us better understand this. The Tormentors asked you to ask us to help them save the one that saved us from them?" the ever cantankerous Thardulma spat, "I find this whole affair thoroughly distasteful. The fact that we are even discussing their proposal is preposterous. How do we know you are not in cahoots with them?!"

The chamber rumbled in agreement.

Thaddraver stood and addressed the grumbling crowd, "While we are indebted to Jett Javelin for restoring the Boonan way of life, we can never forgive or trust those demons who stole so much from us. I, for one, move to reject their plea."

The fellow Parliamentarians shouted their approval.

"There will be no help for The Tormentors!" one cried.

"Let them find another pawn for their game!"

"I lost everything to The Darkness! To Tarrevel with them!"

The chamber erupted with hoots and applause. Tii-Eldii stood silently as the vitriolic banter escalated and waited patiently for the clamor to die down. When the fulminations finally ceased, all eyes were on him. Distrust and anger were painted on nearly every face confronting in the great chamber.

While Tii-Eldii agreed to help the Aaptuuans, he knew it was going to be very difficult to convince his brethren to do the same. There was no love lost for The Fold and memories of The Great Darkness were still fresh in the popular memory. As far as the average Boonan was concerned, The Fold was the manifestation of evil itself, and most still lived in fear that one day it would cast the planet back into darkness.

"Fellow Boonans, I am not blind to your hatred of The Tormentors as I share much of it myself. However, let us not forget who they are asking us to save. After I left Boona in one of the twelve arks with my friend, Ripeem, who was later tragically lost to the infinite darkness of space, I spent almost a century alone on the dusty red world of Lanedaar 3. My isolation helped me to come to terms with what The Fold had done to us and our once sprawling interplanetary empire. When we reflect upon our own history of conquest," Tii-Eldii said gesturing to war murals that still decorated the ceiling and walls of the vast chamber, "and those civilizations we destroyed and enslaved without a second thought, not mourning their losses, but rather celebrating our victories... The Great Boonan Empire was built upon the backs of those creatures unlucky enough to inhabit the ever-expanding radius of our ambition. Shouldn't we have required The Ten Laws of Civilized Living to apply to all species? And furthermore, why did we require the Ten Laws to instruct us not to behave like savages? The Aaptuuans could have easily wiped us from existence, but they did not. Rather, they forced us to mature as a civilization by allowing us to reexperience life at the bottom of the food chain. While you may not realize it, The Fold answers to a higher authority which it calls The Great White Light. The Fold, itself, is a pawn in an even greater game."

Tii-Eldii paused and allowed those gathered to consider his remarks.

"You defend them? They murdered untold billions and caused a century of suffering for the Boonan people. Not a soul among us can say they haven't lost someone to The Great Darkness," Thardulma argued, "You, Tii-Eldii, lost much of your own family even as you suffered in exile on a desolate planet. How can you now ask us to help them?"

Tii-Eldii stood quietly for a few moments until the chamber became silent as a cemetery at midnight.

Then he said, "I only ask because it is Jett. He is why I am home. It is Jett who brought an end to The Great Darkness. Now Jett and his planet stand on the razor's edge of a great apocalypse. Do we Boonans forget our honor? Do we Boonans no longer repay our debts? The Fold asks only for 10,000 volunteers. Jett Javelin saved 3,000,000,000 of us! Will not 10,000 Boonans answer the call?"

"How can we trust The Tormentors?" shouted one.

"The Fold is not forcing our hand. They have promised to keep things as they are regardless of our decision in this matter. But time is of the essence. If we do not come to the aid of Solaris, it is unlikely anyone will and Jett Javelin will perish."

"Very well," said Thaddraver, "We must never forget our debt or our honor. While I believe your quest is a foolhardy one, and I will never trust The Tormentors, you, Tii-Eldii, seem swayed by their entreaty. I move that if Tii-Eldii can find ten thousand Boonans as foolish as himself, we should allow them to fight for our honor. They must be made aware that this is likely a suicide mission perpetrated by our oppressors whose motives remain unknown, purportedly in the name of our great savior. All in favor?"

The chamber burst out in a cacophony of argument as the yeses and noes made their cases. After much posturing, horse trading, speech making, outright cursing, and careful vote count, the motion narrowly passed the chamber.

"The Ayes, have it," Thardulma announced, "I pray, Tii-Eldii, that you are not undertaking a fool's errand. Are there any volunteers among us here who are brave enough to embark on this quest?"

"I volunteer," Tii-Eldii replied.

The members of the chamber looked at each other and surveyed the room as if to dare one another to raise a claw. A few awkward minutes passed, but, other than Tii-Eldii, there was not a single volunteer. Tii-Eldii glared out into the crowd.

"Cowards... When Jett Javelin risked his life and planet for us, none of you batted an eye. Are you so frightened by The Fold that you would forfeit one of our most prized virtues? You are a pathetic lot! So much for honor..."

The crowd mumbled and stirred uncomfortably in their seats.

Thardulma stepped up to Tii-Eldii and said, "I am afraid you have your answer. Unless you go alone, The Tormentors will receive no help from Boona."

Chapter 19
Bigfoot Begins

Maria and her mother emerged from the far end of the old moonshiners' tunnel and into the dark frozen Canadian wilderness. The pursuing agents were now hundreds of yards behind them and on the other side of an international boundary, but there would be no time to rest, they would stop at nothing to capture Maria. Soon heavily armed operatives would be scouring these woods in search of the two fugitives.

"Mom, it's freezing out here," Maria complained.

"I know, sweetie. Hopefully your dad put some warm stuff in these packs."

Bella rested her back on a nearby log and began rifling through her pack. She pulled out a hat, gloves, and a light fleece jacket.

"Here, put these on," she said as she proceeded to search Maria's pack where she found a matching set of winter clothing which she immediately put on, "I'm afraid we're a little light on warm clothes, but it's better than nothing. There are some road flares in here, when we are far enough away, we can light a fire."

"I'm still cold."

"I know. We can light a fire soon. I promise. If we keep moving, we'll warm up."

"Which way should we go?"

"Let's go this way. Come on, hurry, the faster we go, the warmer we'll be."

The frozen ground crackled under their feet, creating a racket that echoed through the woods. Maria worried that the bad men would hear all the noise, but no matter how carefully she trod, the ground continued to crunch under every step. Her joints began to ache as the bitter cold penetrated her clothing, and her eyeballs felt as though they would frost over at any moment.

"Mama, we have to stop and light a fire. It's soooo cold," she shivered.

Her mother stopped and removed her fleece jacket. She handed it to Maria, but Maria just looked at her confused.

"C'mon, now. Put it on!"

"But, Mama, what about you?"

"I'll be fine. Put it on. We have to keep moving. It's only a matter of time before they find the other end of that tunnel. When that happens, we need to be as far away as possible.

As they continued to trudge on, Maria could see by the expression on her mother's face, that she was struggling to keep warm. She constantly rubbed her arms and blew into her hands. Maria knew her mother would refuse to take the jacket back, so all she could do was hope that they could light a fire soon, but, with the men in pursuit, that seemed increasingly unlikely.

The pair continued northward; Maria continuously looked over her shoulder in paranoia. There were fleeting movements between the trees that caught the corners of her eyes, but when she looked directly at them, there was nothing there. She didn't know what kind of animals lived in these vast woods, but whatever she thought she saw, it was enormous, and its presence provided her with an additional incentive to hasten her pace. She hoped they weren't being stalked by a cougar or a grizzly. Her dad had told her stories of the grizzlies that inhabited these woods. They had names like Smokey Joe, Bone-crusher, and Widow-maker, and Maria had no interest in meeting any of them up close.

The sound of dogs barking rose in the distance.

"Mom? Are those wolves?"

"I'm afraid not, they sound like hunting dogs. They're onto us. C'mon baby, we have to hurry."

Bella grabbed Maria by the hand and pulled her along. Maria struggled to keep up and fell several times.

"Sweetie, I know it's hard, but you have to keep going. Trust me, it will be a lot harder if they catch us."

The dogs' baying grew louder. Now when Maria peered back over her shoulder, she saw flashlights streaming through the trees and heard the sounds of male voices calling to each other. She looked up at her mother whose face wore a look of dogged determination as she dragged her daughter through the icy wilderness. When she turned again to assess the agents' progress, she saw a massive shadowy silhouette. The enormous creature stood on two legs, like a person, only it was significantly taller and shaggier than any person Maria had ever seen. The creature quickly disappeared again into a thicket of trees just as Maria and Bella emerged onto an open meadow.

"What are you staring at, Maria? Hurry up!"

"Mom, there's something following us."

"Yeah, that's why we have to go faster! Half the CIA is chasing us!"

A sudden burst of light filled the clearing. The sound of helicopter engines and shouting men surrounded them. Bella was shot in the leg with a dart and collapsed to the ground.

"Sorry, sweetie. I tried. I really tried," she cried through her tears before becoming unconscious.

A deep voice rumbled in Maria's head, "Run!"

Without a thought, she dropped Bella's hand and sprinted for the darkness that lay just beyond the meadow's edge. She ran headlong into the shadow of the tree line and was immediately lifted off the ground. Agents converged from the opposite end of the clearing and began shouting orders at Bella.

"Stay on the ground," one barked.

"Keep your hands where we can see them!"

"Where's the girl?"

"She ran that way!"

Wind and branches rushed past Maria's face as she was ferried away at tremendous speed by the dark, damp, and musky shadow. All sounds of human activity quickly faded. Not sure of who or what had seized her, she tentatively glanced up at her abductor.

In the darkness, she had trouble making it out its features, but the creature's face was more human than ape, with a large sloping forehead and flat pig like nose. Other than its face, practically every inch of its body was covered in thick, dark, and rank smelling hair.

She panicked and attempted to free herself, but the creature was unrelenting. She wanted to run back and help her mother, but it was no use. What did this creature want with her? Was it hungry? Struggle though she might, she was no match for the monster's brute strength.

Eventually, her exhaustion overwhelmed her, and the rocking motion of the creature's gate coupled with the warmth of its fur, lulled her to sleep. When she awoke the next morning, she lay on a thin mattress on the floor of a sparse log cabin. The red orange light of dawn streamed in through the cabin's single dusty window. She cautiously stood up and walked to it to get her bearings. As she peered through the window, the floor of the cabin began to rock back and forth violently. She was thrown against the far wall and doused with cold water.

When she opened her eyes, waves splashed against the porthole windows of what appeared to be a boat. Her body pitched to and fro and water soaked her as waves washed over the top of the vessel and through the hatch above her.

"Get off your lazy ass, Maria! We need you topside. Storm's picking up!" Jack bellowed through the hatch, "all hands on deck!"

Maria smiled. She was grateful. It wouldn't be long now.

Chapter 20
Topsy Turvy

Maria ascended the ladder up to the deck where she was greeted by a violent fomenting sea. Cyd clung to a teak handrail with one hand while she frantically strapped down their provisions with the other. Brother Duc fought the ship's wheel to keep the small boat on course as waves smashed against the hull and spilled over the railings and down into the hold.

"Maria!" Brother Duc shouted, "Close and secure that hatch! We can't afford to have any more water go below deck! We're getting low on fuel and don't need the extra weight! Plus, no sense in sinking! We're less than an hour from Eureka!"

The wind howled in their faces, constantly changing direction as the waves tossed them about through the thick fog.

Then, as suddenly as it began, the storm switched off. The darkness receded and the howling wind faded to a whisper. Only the cool foggy mist remained. The boat settled down into foamy waves that radiated outward from the boat in concentric circles, as if someone had tossed a giant boulder into the ocean.

"I don't get it," said a dumbfounded Jack, "Is that how storms work on the ocean? I've never seen a storm like that before."

Cyd and Brother Duc both stared at Maria, then Brother Duc abruptly broke the silence, "Probably just a localized cell. Not uncommon this time of year."

"Don't B.S. me! Why are you looking at her like that? Did she do this?"

Brother Duc continued, "Like I said, localized cell."

"I found a can of gas. Where do I pour it?" Maria asked.

"Don't worry about it, I'll take care of it," Brother Duc offered, "Why don't you sit down and try to relax."

"Relax? Really? How can anyone *relax* around you people?"

Brother Duc ignored Jack, gently retrieved the gas can from Maria, and emptied it into the tank, "Well, that's the last of it."

"Good thing we're so close," Maria said turning her attention to unstrapping the provisions and packs Cyd worked so hard to secure moments earlier.

Duc nodded. Cyd looked away to avoid making any eye contact with Jack who stood there annoyed, waiting for the punchline.

"What's going on?" he pressed, "You guys aren't telling me something."

"The storm is over and that's all that matters at the moment," Brother Duc answered, "If I were you, Mr. Javelin, I would worry less about the storm that has passed and focus more on the storm to come."

"Like Hazbog?"

"There are far more powerful forces in the universe than Hazbog. You will need to look past him if you ever hope to find your brother," the monk warned.

"Huh? What's that supposed to mean?"

"There's our spot!" Maria called, "It's over there by that giant rock," she pointed to a promontory poking through the fog like a dragon's claw.

"Cyd, gather up all you need and put everything else in that black bag," Duc pointed, "so I can toss it all overboard. Jack, you might want to start looking a little prettier," he smiled, tossing Jack his discarded feminine disguise, "Just kidding, you can keep the fatigues and boots as a gift from me."

A man's voice came over the radio:

Attention all ships in the Eureka area. Be on the lookout for a small vessel that is reported to be in the area. It was last seen off the coast of

Santa Cruz heading north. The vessel is suspected to be carrying two males and two females who are known fugitives. They are thought to be armed and extremely dangerous. If you see this vessel or one resembling it, you are to remain at a safe distance and report the sighting immediately to the United States Coast Guard."

"Well, ladies and gentlemen, looks like we're about to have some company. Time for you three to get scarce."

Chapter 21
Landfall

The clouds were parting behind Brother Duc as he tossed the last backpack to Jack, who stood knee deep in the cold frothy surf. Maria and Cyd quickly organized the rest of their provisions further up the mist enshrouded beach, just inside the tree line where they were less likely to be spotted by helicopter and drone sensors as the fog burned off.

"Thanks, Brother Duc for aiding and abetting my kidnappers on this unexpected journey."

"First of all, you're not a kid and, second of all, you haven't been napped. They really are just trying to help you, you know ...and your brother. They are telling the truth."

"And why am I supposed to trust you?"

"You wouldn't have come this far if you didn't believe them. You can walk away anytime," Duc smirked, "or swim if you like," he chuckled.

"Ha-ha. Well, I've come this far and if Hazbog really is looking for me, I better make myself scarce."

"And you just might find your brother."

"Yeah, I'm not there yet."

Jack looked through the parting fog, past Brother Duc, and saw several boats converging at the horizon.

He pointed to them and shouted, "Boats! We need to get out of here!"

Brother Duc craned his neck and saw them there too. The growing engine noise caught Maria's attention who popped up and gestured emphatically at Jack to get off the beach.

"Tell the girls not to worry," Brother Duc waved, "I got this. Get as deep into those woods as you can. Hurry!"

"What about you?"

"Don't worry about me. I still have a quarter tank of gas and these," he said pulling two fully dressed dummies out of a starboard hold, "I'll give you a head start. Now get out of here!"

Jack nodded and, sprinting up the beach, shouted to the girls, "Go! Go! Go!"

The three disappeared into the thick emerald forest, and Brother Duc threw the throttle forward, taking boat out to sea.

"He's really something," Jack called.

"He's giving us a fighting chance," Maria yelled, "C'mon, there's no time!"

They pushed their way through the thick ferns and underbrush until they found a game trail leading to a wildlife underpass that took them under Highway 101 and deep into the wilderness. The dense canopy of trees kept them safely out of view from prying eyes in the sky. Maria stopped briefly now and again to consult her maps or look at her compass, but they talked very little as they pressed onward through the fragrant misty forest for several miles.

"Can we take five?" he asked after what felt like eternity, "I think we lost 'em."

"We need to get about another mile or so up this ridge," Maria huffed.

"Seriously?" Jack complained, "If the middle of nowhere, had a middle of nowhere, that'd be here," he announced, making a large X with the heel of his boot in the muddy red soil.

"Just a little further, Jack. No pain, no gain," Cyd forced an exhausted smile.

Jack decided it best to push on without further complaint. What was another mile at this point?

For the past several hours, he had been reflecting on his current predicament. Kidnapped by two crazy chicks. Thrust into another situation where he might get killed or worse, and by now, he was pretty tired of almost getting killed, especially by aliens. Of course, it could've been worse, at least there was no blood mist to contend with.

In the nearly three years or so since his brother's disappearance, Jack spent much time reflecting on the events that led up to and took place on Alipour. The bloodmist remained the most terrifying creature he had ever encountered, but he would gladly face a thousand bloodmists if it meant he would see Jett again.

In the early days, he'd often pray for Jett's safe return home, but eventually, Jack had to face the fact that it wasn't ever going to happen and came to accept his brother's passing. Why couldn't Cyd do the same? Why was she so insistent that Jett was still alive? What would they find at the end of this crazy trip?

"Wait, do you hear that?" Cyd asked in a hushed voice, grabbing Jack's arm.

"What?"

"Shhh! That buzzing... Do you hear it?"

Jack listened carefully. He could make out a soft robotic buzzing above the usual sounds of the forest.

"Yeah, it almost sounds like..."

"Drone swarm!" Maria warned, "We have to hide."

The three darted off the narrow path and into the damp underbrush where they found a large tree that had toppled over a boulder. They scurried underneath it. Maria grabbed several branches off the forest floor and used them to cover the entrance. She quickly smeared mud all over her face and arms. She instructed Cyd and Jack to do the same, telling them that it would mask their heat signatures. They laid flat and silent in that muddy hole for some time.

"I think we lost them," Jack said.

"Quiet!" Maria scolded, "Listen..."

Jack closed his eyes and listened intently. He peered up into the tree canopy. In an opening between the branches where the sun shined through, he could see a dark cloud churning back on itself. He looked at Maria. She nodded holding her finger to her lips.

The cloud descended through the tree branches and, as it did, any leaf, twig, or branch that met it was instantly shredded. What moments earlier sounded like the buzzing of bees became the sterile mechanical hum of dozens of tiny electric motors until the drone swarm hovered just a few meters above their hiding spot.

Now that it was so close, Jack was able to make out at least 50 dragonfly sized drones flying in perfect synchronization. Each was emblazoned with U.S. Army markings.

"Jack Javelin," the drones rang out in unison, "Abcde Queen, and Fugitive #3, this is your only warning. You will come with us peacefully on orders of President Montoya. Come out with your hands in the air."

Jack turned to Maria, "Fugitive #3?"

"What should we do?" Cyd asked.

"We should do as they say," Maria said pushing the branches aside as she stepped out with her hands above her head.

Cyd followed suit and after a slight hesitation, so did Jack.

"What now?" Jack asked.

"Wait for it," Cyd smiled.

Maria pressed her eyelids together and a nearly imperceptible white glow traveled down the sides of her head and neck, over her shoulders, and up into her raised arms. The moment the light reached the outstretched palms of her hands, shockwaves pulsed from her fingertips. They shot up and slammed into the drones, causing them to rain harmlessly down onto the forest floor.

Maria kept her eyes closed for a few more seconds, and, taking a deep breath, said, "They have a lock on our position. There ain't no rest for the wicked."

Jack turned to Cyd, "Where did you find this girl again?"

"No time for that, Jack," Maria pressed, "they know where we are. This way! Quickly!"

Chapter 22
The Honor of Boona

His day of testifying before the council had left Tii-Eldii drained.

"Their behavior is appalling," he growled, "if not for Jett Javelin they'd still be wallowing around in the dark. Pathetic. Ungrateful. Dishonorable..." he yawned.

As he leaned forward in his chair, memories of Jett raced through his mind. He recalled their chance meeting in the dusty red desert of Lanedaar 3 and his crunchy lunch of charlatones. He chuckled softly, cradled his exhausted head in a soft bed of tentacles, and fell fast asleep on his desk.

He rode again in the sticky pouch of his favorite pocket worm, Märta, through miles of tunnels toward his hidden ark and its loyal guardian, the crab monster, Craabic.

"I guess you get used to the smell," came a voice, "eventually..."

"Who is that?"

Tii-Eldii felt something take hold of his claw and pull on it through the pouch.

"Jett? Is it you?"

"In this place, at this moment in time, it is me."

"Jett, I am sorry."

"For what?"

"I am sorry I could not convince my people to help your planet."

"I'm sure you did everything you could. And don't worry, we'll see each other again very soon. Now wake up! Wake up! Wake up, Tii-Eldii!"

Tii-Eldii sat straight up in his chair.

"Tii-Eldii, wake up, you have to see this! C'mon, hurry!" Ekiwoo called.

Tii-Eldii groggily rose from his chair, trying to shake off the dream, and followed Ekiwoo into the other room where a monitor blared:

"Tens of thousands of Boonan volunteers have gathered around the habitation tower of renowned scientist and Boonan hero, Tii-Eldii, ready to sacrifice their lives for Solaris 3. Thousands of similar gatherings are being reported across Boona. Many have called it a suicide mission, but for those volunteering, it is a matter of honor. Let us go to At-Räm who is on the ground at the tower's main entrance. At-Räm, what are these brave souls telling you?"

"The volunteers are very excited to repay one of Boona's greatest heroes, Jett Javelin. The support here is overwhelming and demonstrates more than anything the sense of honor we Boonans hold so dear. Sir, why are you here?"

"I lost many friends to The Great Darkness, and I myself almost succumbed, but Jett Javelin gave me a second chance. He gave us all a second chance. It was the second chance our planet may not have deserved, but desperately needed. If I can do for Jett a fraction of what he did for me... us... it would be my great honor."

"Thank you. Madam, how about you?"

"We Boonans have integrity. It is the foundation of our great civilization. It is shameful that none on the council share our conviction. I believe in what Boona has become since Jett and Tii-Eldii chased away The Darkness. I believe this is our chance to prove to ourselves and The Tormentors how far we've come, that we are truly deserving of the second chance we've been given."

"Thank you, Madam. At-Räm signing off."

"Thank you, At-Räm. Now turning to..."

Tii-Eldii ran out onto his balcony and peered down into the courtyard. A massive crowd ebbed and flowed beneath him. When they spotted Tii-Eldii hanging over his railing, they erupted in loud bellowing cheers. Ekiwoo joined him outside and waved down to her husband's admirers.

"Tii-Eldii they are all here because of you."

Tii-Eldii looked at Ekiwoo and said, "He was right."

"Who?"

"Nothing. Look at that! Can you believe it?" he turned to address the crowd, "with this resurgent spirit, Boona will rise again. The best and brightest among you will join our mission to repay our debt by standing with our brothers on Solaris 3."

The crowd roared.

"With so many volunteers, surely you will not need to go," Ekiwoo argued.

"How can I ask them to risk their lives, if I am not willing to do the same? I am as prepared to go alone as I am to go with a million of my brothers and sisters," he turned again to the crowd, "onward to Solaris 3!"

Chapter 23
Running with the Devil

Hazbog poked his long-clawed finger at his scaly forearm. As he did, a fleshy hole opened, and its circumference glowed with a diffused blue light. He pressed his finger further and further in until it passed through to the other side. He held his arm up in disbelief, examining it from every possible angle.

"So, it's begun," an unannounced visitor commented.

"Who dare!?!" Hazbog barked and spun around to meet the intruder, "Oh, it's you..."

"You sound disappointed to see me, Hazbog," the Eelshakian General Ripeem smirked, "Is this how you treat your guests? It's no wonder you have so few friends."

"What do you want?" Hazbog snarled.

"I'm just checking on your progress. The last time we visited, you were demonstrating with great competence how to fail in every conceivable way. And so, with such a track record I hesitate to ask - have you found the boy?"

"Always with the boy. While I've made it perfectly clear why I must find him," Hazbog spat, "What's not so clear is why he is important to you. Do you care to enlighten me?"

"Word of the boy's invention is spreading throughout the galaxy like wildfire. A boy with his kind of reputation will fetch a high price. There are many enemies of The Fold who would relish the opportunity to use his technology against it. I would simply love to be able to aid them in their endeavors."

"What about me?" Hazbog challenged.

"We have a deal. You will be fairly compensated for your efforts and will have time to download his knowledge of the machine to use for whatever purposes you wish. That is, if you and your goons are ever able to finish the job."

"We are close. We'll have his brother and friends in custody very shortly. We've pinpointed their location and my Alipouran henchmen are tightening the noose."

"That's the first encouraging thing you've told me."

Hazbog grunted and then asked, "Ripeem, what did you mean before?"

"I don't follow."

"What did you mean when you said that it's begun? What's begun?"

"Quantum sickness. Your subatomic bonds have been disassembled and reassembled so many times, that you are randomizing. It always starts in the extremities but will consume your entire body until you are trapped in the in-between. The space between space. There's no stopping it now. Unless..."

"Unless what?"

"Unless we obtain a quantum containment suit. It so happens that Jett Javelin is in possession of such a thing."

"How do you know this?" Hazbog growled.

"A person of my talent knows many things, some might say most things. Why don't we do this. I'll up the ante. If you get me Jett by my next visit, I'll not only pay you what I promised, but I'll let you have a close look at that suit of his so you can reverse engineer one for yourself."

Hazbog considered the traveler's new offer. It was rumored that Jett suffered from a malady related to overuse of his machine. Could it be the same quantum sickness that afflicted him? Hazbog wondered how many swaps he might have left before he vaporized completely and permanently. Ripeem seemed to believe that quantum sickness was irreversible, but if he stopped swapping entirely would it slow down or stop its progression? He resolved then and there that he would now take a shuttle to and from the planet's surface and set up a field office in Washington DC to minimize his comings and goings until such a time he was ready to leave the planet for good.

"If I had a suit of my own, could I continue swapping?"

"I don't see why not."

"Excellent," Hazbog sneered.

"Only, you need to have him here by my next visit, or the deal's off," Ripeem warned.

"When can I expect you next?"

"Soon," Ripeem smiled and abruptly vanished.

Chapter 24
Big Shoes to Fill

"Seriously, are you a Jedi?" Jack asked in amazement as he examined the defunct drones scattered in the undergrowth, "the car, the storm, and now this. What the hell are you?"

"There's no time for questions. The swarm no doubt reported our location to the authorities before I could take it out. This place will be overrun by federal agents any minute. Hurry!" Maria ordered as she grabbed her pack and darted through the forest.

Jack picked up his stuff and raced after her.

When he caught up to her, he said, "We can walk and talk right?"

"Best to keep it down," Maria whispered, "those drones can pick up the faintest sounds. I'll tell you whatever it is you need or want to know once we we're safe with my friends."

"You have friends out here? Can you communicate with animals, too?"

"Just one," Maria replied, "but they don't consider themselves to be animals in the literal sense. Now keep quiet!" she scolded.

Maria would've liked to have answered Jack's questions, and could certainly understand his confusion, but she didn't feel like she had the answers he was looking for. She really didn't know what she was. What memories she had of her parents were vague and distant. Her only interaction with any humans after her separation from her parents, before Brother Duc found her wandering the northern woods alone, was with the old fisherman who stocked up the remote cabin every summer and gave her books and other things to keep her occupied through the long, dark, cold, and lonely winters.

As far back as Maria could remember, she was able to control objects with her thoughts. This ability made her quite challenging as an infant and toddler. When she would become upset, the shit would literally hit the fan. Fortunately, her father developed a unique gift for soothing her by singing her Beatles songs and in time, he helped her understand how to better control her urges. He made a habit of singing her to sleep every night whether she was having a good day or a particularly bad day. It really didn't matter, her father was always singing to Maria, and his favorite song was Blackbird.

Maria requested the song so often that her father anointed her with it as her nickname. It was the last name he called her before he sent her into the moonshiners' tunnel a lifetime ago.

"How much further?" Cyd whispered.

"We're here," Maria said.

"We're where, exactly?" Jack asked, "the middle of nowhere? Pretty sure that's where we are. In the middle of nowhere being chased by flesh eating drones as Fugitive #3 uses Jedi mind tricks to wreak all sorts of havoc. Did I get that right?"

"Pretty good synopsis, I have to say," Cyd smirked.

"Shhhhhh... quiet... they're here," Maria said.

"Who?" Jack asked.

"I said, shhhhhhhhh!" Maria barked.

Jack shrugged and leaned against a tall redwood tree. He was certain they soon be captured. They hadn't made it too far from where Maria had incapacitated the drone swarm, so it was only a matter of time before the entire army, Hazbog, and God knows what else caught up with them.

Jack saw a large patch of forest floor lifting up from under the giant roots of an enormous redwood tree. He blinked his eyes and took a second look.

"C'mon," Maria whispered, "Go, go, go!"

"Where are we going?"

"We're going underground, Jack. We can't stay up here. I can stop drones, but I can't stop Marines."

"You flipped a car..."

"Jack, enough," Cyd whispered, grabbing his hand and pulling him toward a large root covered doorway that had opened under an enormous redwood tree.

Maria rushed out in front and led them through the opening. The first thing Jack noticed upon crossing the threshold was a strong musky stench that hung thick in the air.

"Whoa!" he winced, "Smells like someone with B.O. ate a pile of onions!"

"Shut up and follow me," Maria ordered.

The large door closed with a thud behind them. Light streamed in through tiny gaps in the tangled roots that made up the roof and walls of the tunnel. Maria led them through a multitude of complex intersecting passages. Jack hadn't seen anyone manning the door and there was no sign of anyone or anything else in the tunnel other than insects and spiders.

Yet out of the corners of his eyes shadows darted about in the darkness of intersecting tunnels as they worked their way along. The size of the tunnels was impressive, and most were high enough to comfortably host the tallest NBA players and wide enough to accommodate a small car. It was hard to imagine that such a large network of tunnels was laying just beneath their feet. Maria stopped suddenly.

"We're here," she announced, "Jack, Cyd, I'd like to introduce you to my friends."

From out of the dark corners and passageways stepped dozens of giant ape men, the tallest of which stood as high as a regulation basketball net. Jack's jaw hung slack as he craned his neck to look up at them.

"Big Mouth meet Bigfoot," Maria smiled.

Cyd grinned, "It's true! It's not like I didn't believe you, but c'mon it's actually Bigfoot! Was a little hard to keep the faith, but here we are. They're kinda like Alipourans, don't you think, Jack?"

"Only smellier," Jack winced, "and a lot bigger."

Maria approached the largest of the group. It cradled her hands inside its enormous palms, and they both bowed their heads.

"What are they doing?"

"They're communicating, Jack. Give them some quiet time."

Jack nervously surveyed the cavern. He guessed there were around fifty of these creatures, but he could hear footsteps and grumbling in the darkness beyond. They were enormous and covered in reddish brown hair that appeared matted and wet. Of course, just as legend had it, their feet were gigantic. After a very awkward and uncomfortable few minutes, Maria bowed again and rejoined her friends.

"What did it say?" Cyd asked.

"Big Red says we are welcome to stay for as long as we like. When we are ready leave, we can use their tunnels to complete the next leg of our journey."

"Is its name really Big Red? Big Red the Bigfoot? You have to be kidding me."

"Jack, in order to pronounce her name correctly, I'd have to pull your tongue out and put it back in the other way," Maria teased, "Loosely translated her name is Mama Big Red. She is queen of the Northern Woods."

"Okay, then, Big Red, when am I going to wake up?"

"She can't understand you, Jack. I can communicate with her because we bonded when I was a young child. A Sasquatch's ability to communicate telepathically is what has allowed it to remain undetected all these years. Just because you've never seen a Bigfoot, doesn't mean a Bigfoot hasn't seen you."

"Okay, I'm trying to follow this, so is Big Red the queen of the Bigfoot?"

"Have a seat, Jack," Maria huffed as she sat down on a large root protruding from the tunnel wall, "Okay, questions. What do you got? I'll tell you everything I know."

Brother Duc slowly regained consciousness. He groaned and tried to sit up, but he was tethered to metal operating table.

"Oh, look who's awake," a voice announced.

"Where am I?"

"You are aboard the Coast Guard cutter Alexander Hamilton off the coast of Eureka, California."

"Who are you?"

"My name is not important, but I would like to introduce you to my commander, Hazbog."

"Wakey, wakey," Hazbog hissed, "We have much to discuss," electric current ran up and down the length of his body, "Why don't we start with your friends..."

Chapter 25
Boe Hunters

"You're saying a teenage girl did this?" a camouflaged marine asked, wide eyed.

"Not any teenage girl," Agent Smith replied, "She's known as Fugitive #3. As far as we know, the girl has no identity, no records, no fingerprints, nothing, but whoever she is, she's not to be trifled with. As you are aware, we are under strict orders to bring her and the others back alive. Sedation will be necessary."

There was a loud rustling in the forest canopy. Smith craned his neck and saw a large contingent of Boe warriors swinging and leaping through the branches as they fanned out across the forest. The ground shook as hundreds more raced across the forest floor. Their hoots and calls echoed back and forth from the forward scouts to the main body of the raucous army which now flooded the area.

"God help those kids if Hazbog's creatures get to them first," Smith commented, "Please see to it that you and your men stay one step ahead of the Boe."

"Sir, we're trying, but you see how fast they are. My best men can't keep pace much less stay ahead."

"I didn't ask to hear excuses."

"Yes, sir," the marine saluted and jogged off to command his unit.

Smith bent down and picked up a single dragonfly sized drone and fiddled with it between his fingers. Its delicate electronics were thoroughly fried, and it was still warm to the touch. Smith placed the drone in his pocket and continued his forensic analysis of the area.

"We will have them soon," Hazbog grinned upon entering the clearing flanked by a half dozen armored Boe bodyguards.

Smith looked up at him and nodded.

"Not much to say, I see. Well, your work here is very important, Solarian, so do it well, for your own sake."

Smith nodded again. Hazbog glanced down at the pile of drones and shrugged. He signaled to the Boe to continue east.

"Strange the power of this girl," Hazbog commented to Smith as he picked up a defunct drone, "This ability of hers is unheard of on Solaris 3 and is rare even in the known galaxy."

"I don't know anything about that," Smith answered dismissively, "All I know is there is no record of this girl's existence. It's possible The Fold brought her here to protect The Javelins, but there's no way of knowing for sure until we find, secure, and interrogate her."

"The girl will need to be neutralized before she can be taken into custody. I have just the thing," Hazbog hissed, holding up a small capsule, "this device will encapsulate her in a psychic field that increases in strength the more she resists it."

"You're planning to use her brain waves against her?"

"The brilliant part is, it's powered by her brain waves," Hazbog replied, "higher intensity translates to higher power."

A loud racket erupted in the forest several hundred yards away from them. Several Boe pivoted and rushed in direction of the sound.

"I believe we may have found our fugitives," Hazbog said cheerfully, "and none too soon."

Big Red beckoned them on through the root and cobweb filled passages. Jack was impressed by how these huge creatures were able to move so nimbly through the tunnels. He found it extremely challenging to keep up with them, especially since he was just catching his breath from the last marathon sprint following the drone incident.

They had been running ever since the Bigfoot troupe had become inexplicably agitated a little while earlier. Maria explained to Jack and Cyd that the Bigfoot had sensed a large number of humans and other beings entering this part of the forest.

"Where are we going, Cyd?" Jack asked, his thighs and calves were on fire.

"As if I know."

"Away," Maria replied, "away from whoever is spooking the Bigfoot."

"The army?"

"Probably. I've never seen them act this way. Whatever is coming is extremely dangerous."

Cyd looked at Jack, "Do you think it's Hazbog?"

"You're the one who thinks he's after me, so let's go with that."

The tunnel started vibrating wildly and continued to increase in intensity. Dirt and rocks rained down on them. Dust clouded their vision and burned their parched throats. This commotion was immediately followed by the thundering of thousands of feet directly above them and accompanied by a cacophony of otherworldly hoots and hollers.

"I know that sound," Jack whispered.

"Believe me now?" Cyd gulped.

"What is it?" Maria asked.

"Boe warriors," Jack said, "lots and lots of them."

The three stopped and did their best to remain silent. Big Red and the other Bigfoot continued on until they disappeared into the labyrinth. Then, without warning, the thundering footsteps abruptly ceased and Boe calls rang out in the tunnel.

"I think they found us…"

Chapter 26
Lost & Found

Being down in this subterranean labyrinth reminded Maria of events from her childhood when she first came to know the Bigfoot. Isolated as she was from the rest of the world for most of her life, Maria had grown accustomed to living alone deep in the untamed wilderness. Other than time spent with the Bigfoot who called these tunnels home, her long bouts of loneliness were interrupted each summer by the old fisherman who arrived by late May carrying supplies to see her through the next winter.

In addition to outfitting her, the old man taught Maria how to fish and trap and make jerky from whatever she managed to catch. He took her to hidden spots where berries of every kind grew in abundance. He showed her where to dig for wild roots and how to make the most out of the edible bounty that surrounded her. Most importantly, he indoctrinated Maria in the life of a mountain man, including how to avoid predators like wolves, bears, and mountain lions that lurked throughout the woods she called home.

The fisherman also told her stories of large hairy apes that frequented the area and had, from time to time, thrown rocks at, vandalized, and otherwise harassed him at his cabin. He told her that all of this stopped after he found her living there. He called Maria his 'lucky charm'.

"They are my friends," she'd tell him, "and they protect and feed me when you're not around. They are watching us right now," she'd point to the tree line.

Evidence of a Bigfoot presence could be found all around the cabin and included hundreds of large bare footprints, clumps of fur clinging to twigs and branches, and scratch marks covering the trees and rocks surrounding the area. Most notable were the large inverted tree trunks that had been driven into the ground, roots up, in a perfect circle around the cabin.

"Those keep the hungry animals away," she explained.

As was his normal routine, the old fisherman would arrive soon after the first spring blooms emerged from the forest floor and the last of the ice melted from the lake feeding the stream that ran alongside the cabin. His arrival would also mark the disappearance of Big Red and her troop, at least visibly, from the area, though there were always signs they were never far away.

Summer was a very exciting time and Maria always counted down the days until the old man arrived. He always brought new books to read and new games for them to play together, neither of which the Bigfoot were particularly good at. Her favorite book was Heart of Darkness, and even at her young age, having lost both her parents to evil men, Maria could relate to the darkness inherent in human nature.

Yet, this summer was different. It had been several weeks since the forest began its spring transformation, still there was no sign of the old fisherman. Maria worried that something bad might have happened to him. Without fresh supplies, she could expect a very long and hard winter ahead. Besides, she longed desperately for human interaction. As the days turned into weeks, Maria's loneliness and boredom became unbearable. As a result, her wanderings from the cabin became longer and wider as she sought out other fisherman or hunters she could befriend.

It was on one of these long explorations, that a fur clad, matted haired, and wild-eyed Maria first set eyes on Brother Duc. He had set up camp alongside a stream on the far edge of the ridge that bordered the valley where she lived. Her intense curiosity drove her to make the journey to Brother Duc's camp daily where she would quietly observe him from the edges of the thick forest surrounding his camp or silently follow him about as he explored the area.

After a couple of weeks of stalking Brother Duc, Maria arrived one day and found the camp unoccupied. She did a cursory check of the area but could find no trace of the mysterious stranger. Once satisfied she was alone, Maria cautiously approached the camp and began rifling through Brother Duc's supplies and gear.

"Nice of you to visit me again," Brother Duc stated matter-of-factly as he emerged from beneath an enclosure of expertly woven leaves and underbrush.

Maria jumped to her feet and attempted to flee into the woods, but Brother Duc was much too fast and seized her by the arm.

"There's no need to be frightened, little one," he said calmly, but the shock of his sudden appearance was too much for Maria to take and she fell to her knees screaming.

The ensuing shockwave sent Brother Duc flying backward into a large maple tree where he hit his head and was knocked unconscious. When he came to, he found himself wrapped in an itchy wool blanket, laying in the dirt next to a roaring fire. Maria sat stiffly on rock nearby staring at him intensely.

Brother Duc stiffly lifted his hand up to his aching head and groaned, "Who are you? Do you live in these woods?"

Maria continued to stare silently at him.

"Can't talk? I've read stories of wild children, but always believed they were just stories, yet here you are. How long have you been out here, I wonder? Are you all alone or are there others?"

Maria cleared her throat so she could use the voice she hadn't had a reason to use in a very long time, and finally croaked, "All alone. The fisherman did not come this year."

"Fisherman?" Duc puzzled.

"Come, I will show you," Maria said, standing up and coxing Duc to follow her, which he did for several miles in silence until they eventually arrived at the small log cabin by the edge of a stream.

Duc followed her inside where he found a tidy space filled with books, animal furs, fishing gears, traps, and a small wood stove.

"You live here by yourself?"

Maria looked down sadly.

"For how long?"

"Since I was seven and the fisherman has visited seven summers. I guess that would make me fourteen."

"You speak well for someone without formal schooling."

"I went to school when I was a younger and the old fisherman taught me the rest."

"Who is this fisherman?"

"He never told me his name, only that he traveled here from a great distance away. He taught me how to survive out here. He brought me food and supplies, but he has not come yet this summer as I hoped and that is how I found you. I was actually looking for him."

"What if he doesn't come back?"

"Big Red will take care of me then."

"Who is Big Red?"

"She is the queen of the forest."

"Where is she?"

"She will be back soon."

"I see," Duc replied incredulously, "Aren't you lonely?"

"Yes..."

"Silly me," he said, "in all the excitement, I forgot to introduce myself. My name is Brother Duc. What do they call you?"

"Maria."

"Maria, who?"

"Just Maria."

"Well, just Maria, would you mind if I moved my camp up here so that we could get to know each other better?"

"I would like that."

Chapter 27
For Whom the Bell Tolls

Maria's goal was to remain elusive, to stay one step ahead, a feat further complicated by the sudden disappearance of the Bigfoot.

For Jack and Cyd, the thought of Boe warriors roaming the forests of Earth made them quiver. Unlike Maria, they both understood too well the threat of the creatures that were chasing them.

"Some friends you got there. Take off at the first sign of trouble," Jack hissed, "Now what are we supposed to do?"

"Keep moving. The troop won't let us down," Maria whispered as she pressed on through the tunnel, "they are regrouping for a counterattack."

Jack stood there befuddled.

"C'mon, what are you waiting for?" Cyd urged.

"Can't Maria just force power the Boe and whatever else is up there? Why do we need to keep running? What are we afraid of?"

"It doesn't work that way. Look, you wouldn't understand. We need to get out of here... You're wasting time!"

Jack frowned and reluctantly followed Cyd through the massive root filled tunnel. The commotion of footfalls followed above them.

"Will somebody please tell me why are we running? They obviously know we're down here."

Cyd skidded to a halt and glared at Jack, "Do you always give up this easily? Jett would keep fighting!"

"I'm not Jett," Jack growled.

"Whatever," Cyd said turning and climbing over a large tangled root, "do what you want. I'm not rolling over for anybody."

Jack huffed and followed Cyd. As soon as he crested the protruding root, he was tossed off it by a deafening boom that shook the tunnel violently. He looked back through the thick dust and saw a huge steel piston had punched a hole through the ceiling.

"Hurry up! They're coming down here!" Jack called, chasing after the others.

He soon caught up to Cyd and Maria who had briefly stopped at a tunnel junction to decide which way to go. There were still no signs of the Bigfoot.

"Maria, they'll be down here any second. What do we do?"

"Cyd, don't worry, the Troop will protect us. They always protect their own. They have a plan. We have to trust them."

"Trust them?" Jack spat, "They're MIA. And where the hell did they go? We're sitting ducks down..."

"Wait," Cyd interrupted, "Do you hear that?"

"Hear what?"

"Hear," Cyd pointed, "that!"

From the gaping hole in the roof poured dozens of shiny metal cylinders.

"They're going to gas us!" Jack shouted.

Cyd shook her head, "No, not quite," she pointed again, "Worse..."

Each of the cylinders split open and out scurried hundreds of spider robots. Instantly the walls, floor, and ceiling swarmed with them. The black mass of spiderbots enveloped the tunnel as it raced toward them.

"This way!" Maria shouted, turning right down the largest of the tunnels.

The three scurried as fast as their legs would carry them, but the spiderbots were far too fast and closed the distance quickly, to the rhythm of a million tiny clanking feet. Jack spotted a light at the far end of the tunnel and reckoned they would soon emerge into the forest where they would most certainly be captured.

Then the first of the spiderbots dropped onto Jack and sunk its hypodermic fangs into his shoulder. He winced, smacked the spiderbot off, and immediately tripped over a protruding root and fell unconscious. The black mass of spiderbots routed around on either side of and above Jack in pursuit of Cyd and Maria.

Then the spiderbots rained down on Cyd, and she, too, was subdued by their venom.

Maria, who was a fair bit ahead of the others, did an about face and raised her hands in the air to fry this armada of spiderbots when something stung her in the arm. Unfazed, she discharged a shockwave. It lit up in a bubble surrounding her and dissipated. She stood there momentarily with a look of disbelief. She tried again in vain, the energy dissipating all around her. She spun around and sprinted for the exit, but the bots soon overtook her, and she was bitten on the ankle.

Fighting her way to the surface, she finally collapsed on the forest floor. All around raged a battle between the Boe and the Bigfoot. Large rocks and stumps were hurled through the air, crushing any Boe who stood in their way. Bigfoot were unceremoniously slaughtered by the Boe's advanced weapons. Maria watched in a dazed horror as the battle receded from her consciousness, she quickly became numb and didn't feel her head hitting the ground as she passed out.

Chapter 28
Shot in the Dark

Preparations for the Solaris 3 mission were swift. Given Hazbog's stranglehold on the inner solar system, there was no time to spare. Several thousand of Boona's best and brightest were deployed to the fourth moon of Solaris 6 where they prepared to be shot in projectiles through the neutralization field toward the red planet of Solaris 4. Once inside the field, they would regroup for their assault on Hazbog and the Boe in their quest to repay their debt to Jett Javelin.

Tii-Eldii performed his final review of the battle plan while Boonan commanders assembled around him. The mission before them was fraught with peril. The Boonans would be fired from propulsion cylinders through the neutralization field, past Solaris 5, and through the asteroid belt. During this time their ships would be without power, propulsion, or navigation abilities until they reached the outskirts of Solaris 4, safely on the other side of the neutralization field. Here they would form offensive armada and bring the war to Hazbog.

The Aaptuuans performed trillions of calculations in search of the safest route through the asteroid field, but there were no guarantees that all the craft would make it through unscathed. To Tii-Eldii, this would be the most harrowing and dangerous part of their mission. He felt proud the Boonan people would sacrifice so much to defend their planet's honor, and he prayed to Thoh for their safe passage through the asteroid belt.

"After completing the calculations, we have determined that these trajectories provide the highest likelihood of success," Le-Wa pointed to a floating holographic map.

"What are the projected losses?" Tii-Eldii asked with concern.

Le-Wa continued, "In the best case, seventy-six percent of the vessels will survive the trip."

"Worst case?"

"One in five."

"18.759 to be exact," Chi-Col said.

Tii-Eldii turned from the map and looked out at his brethren gathering below them, "I don't like those odds..."

"They are as they are and reflect the best available options given the complexity of the challenge," Le-Wa stated.

"Perhaps luck will prevail," Tii-Eldii reflected, "May Thoh protect us."

"It is time," Chi-Col said.

"So it is. I will address my people," Tii-Eldii held his head up and walked out onto a balcony above the landing bay.

He peered down at the brave Boonans assembled in the cavernous hanger. Rather than dwell on odds of success or failure, he instead turned his thoughts to Jett and his bravery in the face of his own personal and existential challenges.

"My fellow Boonans, we have been graced with the honor of repaying a debt so large that many of us believed it could never be properly repaid. Yet here we are, gathered together on a remote moon in a distant solar system on the precipice of a great battle, the winner of which will determine the fate of not only Solaris 3, but possibly the galaxy as a whole. While for many of us, our mission is one of a personal nature, the larger ramifications its success or failure extend far beyond meager Boonan honor. Many of our brethren will perish in our lofty pursuit, but our unwavering courage and tenacity will prevail!"

The crowd erupted in hoots and cheers.

"For Boona!" Tii-Eldii shouted, tentacles extended.

"For Boona!" the army echoed.

"Now, to our bullet pods!"

"For Boona!" the army called out and disbanded to their assigned vessels.

As they filled with Boonans, the bullet pods were each loaded onto large conveyors and fed into one of three propulsion cylinders, much in the same way rounds are fed into a machine gun. The three guns fired in an alternating pattern at the three calculated trajectories. Tii-Eldii was escorted to his pod by Le-Wa and Chi-Col.

"May the Great White Light guide you and your people to victory."

Tii-Eldii nodded and climbed into the pod. In a matter of moments, he, like the others, was fired though the cold darkness of space at extreme velocity just shy of the speed of light. In a few hours, the projectile armada entered the treacherous asteroid belt. Tii-Eldii watched in horror as bullet pods all around him collided with spinning gray rocks of every shape and size, exploding, careening and ricocheting into each other, or spinning off course with no way of self-correcting.

Tii-Eldii's own pod took several direct hits and he was reminded of his narrow escape from Boona in which his friend Ripeem was lost to an unexpected meteor shower. Way back then his mission was to save his own people, this time many Boonans would be lost in the name of another civilization, none had heard of before the arrival of Jett Javelin.

Eventually, after a very bumpy ride, Tii-Eldii's pod emerged at the far end of the asteroid belt. He reached down to the control panel and activated the craft's power systems.

"Navigation and controls functional. All systems operational," the computer chirped.

Tii-Eldii's radio lit up with communications from the other surviving pods.

"Squad 42, reporting."

"Squad 72, reporting."

"Squad 23, reporting."

Tii-Eldii acknowledged each and after all had reported in, he said, "All pods to rendezvous above the north pole of Solaris 4. Take inventory and prepare damage reports. Say a prayer for our brothers who paid the ultimate price."

Tii-Eldii looked out of his cockpit dome at the motley assemblage of damaged pods, many of which had to be towed to the rendezvous point where making repairs of any kind would be difficult. Less than half of the ships had made it through the asteroid belt. What Tii-Eldii had expected would be a strong show of Boonan force, would now limp into battle against a well-fortified Hazbog and his legions of Boe warriors.

Tii-Eldii closed his eyes and thought aloud,

"What have I done?"

Chapter 29
The Great Ironing

When Jack awoke, he was secured to a cold metal table and surrounded by uniformed military personnel. Blinding lights forced him to squint hard as he attempted to determine where he was and whether Cyd and Maria were there with him.

"Lieutenant inform Hazbog that Jack Javelin is conscious," a voice ordered.

"Yes, sir."

"Who is that?" Jack asked, "Where am I? Where are my friends?"

"Your friends are safe and will remain so for as long as you're cooperative. The same can be said for your parents."

"My parents? What do they have to do with any of this?"

"The same thing you have to do with it," the voice continued, "it's not about them or you or your friends."

"Then what's it about?"

"Do I really need to spell it out for you? Let me be clear, no one cares what happens to you. It's your brother we're interested in, and you're going to help us find him."

"Excellent, he's awake," a jubilant Hazbog declared as he entered the room surrounded by Boe warriors. Jack struggled to free himself from his bonds.

"A familiar story," Hazbog continued confidently, "Last time I saw you, you were stuck up a tree while I tossed your brother Jett into the bloodmist. Still blaming yourself for his death, I see. Well, fret not, I come bearing good news. Your brother is alive."

"You're delusional!"

"Am I?

"Yes. Jett's dead, and you're the one who killed him!" Jack pulled against his restraints.

A voice from behind Jack interrupted, "So this is the Tinker's brother. Full of spirit. Will be a shame to have to break him."

"I disagree, Ripeem," Hazbog smirked, "I think it will be rather entertaining," he laughed uproariously.

"Hazbog, you take far too much pleasure in the misery of others," the voice replied.

"I have seen Hazbog's ugly ass up close, but I don't know who you are," Jack said struggled to turn is head toward the voice, "I don't recognize your voice."

Footsteps came around to where Jack could see the mysterious stranger and he said, "I am known by those gathered here as Ripeem and you now know as much about me as you need to, except for one small detail."

"And what's that?"

"While anybody who knows where to look can find your brother, I am the only person who can fix him."

"Do you mean his quantum sickness?"

"That, among other things, but first I need your help."

"If you're so powerful, why do you need my help? Why do you need to keep me tied up?"

Hazbog growled, "We can't afford to have you running off again, now can we? You were hard enough to catch the first time."

"Tell me where my friends are."

"Of course, how rude of us," Ripeem continued, "the one you call Maria is sedated in the next room. She is far too excitable, um dangerous, to remain conscious. Bring in the other one," he ordered.

Jack turned his head toward the door where a shackled Cyd was led in.

"Cyd, are you okay?"

"Yeah, mostly," she replied, "I still have a bit of a headache from the spiderbot venom and my handcuffs are a little tight. Other than that, I'm loving the five-star service Hazbog and his cronies are providing."

Hazbog grabbed Cyd by the arm and pulled her close to him, "Just like old times," he laughed, "now that we are all together, let's settle this and get down to the business of finding Jett."

"I already told you we don't know where he is," Cyd spat.

"She's telling the truth," Jack concurred.

"And we believe you," Ripeem said, "we didn't bring you here because of what you do or do not know."

"Then why are we here?" Cyd asked.

Hazbog smiled broadly, "When your prey proves impossible to catch, one must lay a trap."

"So, we're the bait, then?"

"Precisely, only here's the rub: Jett isn't going to simply show up if we treat you well, so expect for things to get a little rough. Apologies in advance," Hazbog smirked.

"What's that supposed to mean?" Jack growled.

"More on that later," Ripeem answered smoothly, "Right now we have a press conference to attend," he then turned to several orderlies and said, "please see to it that our guests keep quiet during the broadcast."

"Yes, sir!"

The orderlies took Cyd and Jack and simultaneously stuffed a rubber ball in each of their mouths and covered it with Duct tape. Cyd was led in shackles and Jack was rolled on his examination table into an adjacent room where a battery of television cameras was lined up. Hazbog, Ripeem, the Boe contingent, and a number of military officers, wearing black uniforms that sported an 'iron' patch on their right shoulder, followed them in and lined up in an organized fashion all around them.

Hazbog stepped to the front and began his speech.

"Citizens of Solaris 3, with the capture of Jack Javelin and his band of criminals, we are one step closer to freeing your planet from the tyranny of The Fold. Joining me here today are the brave men and women of The Iron. It was through their untiring efforts that we were able to locate these fugitives and bring them to justice! Thank you for your service. Soon we will have Jett Javelin, The Tinker, in custody. Once this is accomplished, your planet will be free of The Fold forever!"

The Iron officers cheered and The Boe warriors raised their weapons over their heads and hooted wildly.

"Together we will usher in a new age, an age of prosperity for all. Together we will make Earth great again!"

The cheers continued.

"But we are not out of danger yet. The Fold will not yield so easily. Their agents work and live among you. We must root them out and neutralize them before they can undermine our journey to freedom. I encourage all of you to join the brave men and women of The Iron in ushering in a new and better age for all Solarians. If you are not with us, you are against us! Go out now and round up Fold loyalists. Internment camps have been established in every major city. Bring the loyalists there and you will be rewarded! Make Earth great again!"

Chapter 30
Visions of Chaos

Hazbog grinned broadly and waved to the cheering crowd from the ramp of his flagship vessel. The victorious general had brought another resource rich planet under the dominion of the great Eelshakian empire. The swelling throng of his countrymen waved flags and banners in tribute to him.

Scanning the assembly before him, Hazbog recognized the many comrades, concubines, and career politicians who constantly sought to steal credit for his great accomplishments. Yet among those in attendance, was a disturbing anomaly, a Solarian. It stood at the very end the front row and was too far away for Hazbog to make out any details.

His squinting harder to discern who this individual was caused the entire front row to shift to the same Solarian being. This was immediately followed by the next row and the next until the entire mob morphed into the same Solarian boy.

Hazbog felt bewildered and tried to speak out, but no matter how hard he pushed, no sound exiled his throat. He was mute. It was then that the first rock smacked him squarely in the forehead. More rocks followed, thrown by the unruly mob, and rained down on him from every angle.

This was accompanied by the Solarians chanting, "Chaos will reign! Chaos will reign…"

Hazbog remained mute as the volley of rocks continued and intensified along with the chanting. A hand fell on his shoulder. Hazbog spun around and came face to face with the very Solarian he'd been hunting across the galaxy's expanse.

"You're being played," Jett smirked.

Hazbog was unable to speak or move. He watched helplessly as Jett grabbed him violently by the throat and lifted him over the screaming crowd, which had converged beneath them, angrily outstretching their hands to snatch him from Jett's grasp.

"You think I'm the enemy," Jett stared into Hazbog's eyes, "but you are sadly mistaken," he warned before hurling Hazbog into the sea of grasping hands.

"Only three light years remaining," Tii-Eldii said.

"It will be good to be home again," Ripeem grinned, "and you thought The Darkness would never be lifted."

"There is so much I've missed. To be with Ekiwoo again. That is a dream I've dreamed for many long years."

Ripeem agreed, "And a dream that will soon come to pass, as all dreams must eventually, including the one you are currently experiencing as you orbit Solaris 4."

Tii-Eldii looked up in disbelief. Solaris 4? Where had he heard that name before? He looked up at Ripeem, but his old friend was replaced by a tall lanky figure dressed in a long black cloak. Its head was completely hidden in the folds of its shadowy hood.

"Don't I know you?" Tii-Eldii asked, reaching for the being's hood and pulling back it back to reveal a familiar face.

"You used to," Jett remarked, "but much has changed."

"Jett, what happened to you?"

"Chaos will reign."

"What do you mean? What chaos?"

"It is not as it seems... This..."

"Jett, I do not understand what you are talking about. Help me understand."

"Chaos will reign. You are being played."

"Played? By who?"

"Chaos. Chaos rules all."

"Are you coming? The game's about to start."

"I'll be out in a minute," Jack replied, "Just need to get my skates on."

Jack reached down to lace up his hockey skates and saw a pair of worn black boots covered in red mud on the locker room floor in front of him. He lifted his eyes to a monk in long black robe standing there before him.

"What are you doing in here? Spectators aren't allowed in the locker room."

The monk didn't reply, but instead continued to stand silently as a translucent red mist seeped out of the ventilation ducts.

"I said you're not supposed to be in here!"

The monk pulled back his hood.

"Oh my God! Jett, you're alive! I wouldn't let myself believe it no matter how much Cyd tried to convince me."

Jett cocked his head to one side but didn't respond.

"Jett, what are you doing?"

There was no response.

Jack stood up and cautiously took a step toward his brother, "C'mon Jett, buddy. Where have you been? I thought the blood mist killed you."

Jett locked eyes with Jack, "It did," he stated.

"Then how are you here? Why are you dressed like that?"

Jett locked eyes with Jack and said, "Chaos will reign," and as he said this, red mist flowed from his sleeves, and out of the lockers, and in from hallway.

Jack stared in horror as he was once again surrounded by the bloodmist that had consumed his brother and nearly killed him.

"You are all being played," Jett declared before being consumed by the billowing red gas.

Jack's own screams were choked by the noxious mist.

Hazbog, Tii-Eldii, and Jack all simultaneously sprung awake with the same onerous words echoing in their brains: *Chaos will reign...*

Chapter 31
Tomorrow & Tomorrow

"Hazbog, you seem distracted," Ripeem began, "With Jack Javelin and his co-conspirators firmly in our hands, I would think you'd be jubilant. Instead, you are carrying yourself like a neglected puppy."

Hazbog looked up from behind the oversized mahogany desk where he sat reflectively. The previous night's dream was still fresh in his mind. What if this mysterious being standing before him was the very architect of the chaos his dream portended? While Ripeem appeared to Hazbog as an Eelshakian admiral, Hazbog knew that what he saw before him was nothing more than an elaborate illusion designed to ingratiate the creature to Hazbog. No, he understood that whatever this being was, it had a very specific agenda, and that he was but a pawn in its grand scheme.

"Hazbog, do you hear me?"

Hazbog narrowed his eyes, "Yes, I hear you, but now I'm listening. Please indulge me. Can I ask you why you are here?"

"You know quite well why I'm here."

"That's right, you are here to tell me that our deal is off, that there is no quantum suit for me, and that my body will continue to phase in and out of existence until I am finally no more. Is that it?"

Ripeem smiled, "So dour, so negative, it's no wonder you are mired in endless internal strife. You need to lighten up, my friend. With the acquisition of Jack, we are close to achieving our goal, so close in fact, that I'm willing to extend my generous terms. So, tell me, how do you intend to use the Javelin brother to locate the Tinker?"

Hazbog, though still highly incredulous of the being's intentions, perked up a bit at this unexpected turn of events, "As you are aware, the entire planet knows Jack and his accomplices are in custody. Jett is the final piece of the puzzle. The fools believe that their planet has been enslaved by The Fold. They will bring Jett to me to secure their emancipation from their evil Fold overlords," he guffawed, "we will have him in no time."

"And you think they will just turn the Tinker over to you?"

"Of course, they will. Even now, the internment camps are brimming with Fold loyalists betrayed by their own cohort. It is a beautiful thing!" Hazbog chortled, "To harbor Jett Javelin would be treasonous, punishable by, dare

I say it, death, or as the Solarians now know it: 'unlife'!"

"Still, I imagine that the Tinker has many supporters among the populace, and still many more who question whether The Fold is the tyrannical overlord you and your propaganda machine make it out to be. May I suggest a more aggressive approach."

"What do you have in mind?"

"Why don't you place his brother on display? Let's do, I don't know, something fun, dramatic, where he's slowly pulled apart by some crude implement. Multicast his excruciating torture across all media. And to really give the whole affair some pizzazz, I'd recommend a clever device from one of Solaris 3's darker chapters. I believe it is called The Rack. I've located such a device at a place the Solarians call Smithsonian. If the Tinker is anywhere where he can witness his brother's suffering, he will not be able to resist the urge to come running to his rescue, again..."

"And what if this plan of yours fails?"

"I have dealt you a very strong hand, but success is never guaranteed. You will only be defeated if the forests themselves rise up against you," Ripeem smirked.

"All the creatures of Solaris quake in my presence. None shall rise. If any do, they will be immediately and mercilessly dispatched," Hazbog snarled, "I will have the Boe acquire this rack device. Let's ready the cameras."

Chapter 32
Long Live The King

"And we now go live to Dan Howard in Washington D.C. who has the latest on the global search for Jett Javelin. Dan, welcome to the show."

"Thank you, Barbara. Happy to be here in humble service to our esteemed leader. Long live Hazbog."

"Long live Hazbog. Dan, we couldn't help but to notice your friends standing behind you."

"Who? These handsome guys?" Dan replied, as he motioned to armed Boe warriors flanking him on either side, "They follow me everywhere and I am better for it. All love Hazbog."

"Yes, indeed. All love Hazbog. Have you learned anything about Jett Javelin's whereabouts?"

"Well, Barbara, although most people, including his own brother, believe Jett Javelin to be deceased, our beloved leader Hazbog insists he is alive, so therefore, logically he must be so. Currently, millions of 'volunteers', led by Iron operatives, are scouring the planet and leaving no stone unturned in their effort to locate the missing Tinker. Hazbog's representatives at The Iron have taken Jett's parents, his brother Jack

Javelin, and the co-conspirators into custody. As I understand it, interrogations are ongoing. Praise Hazbog."

"All love Hazbog. We all agree that their apprehension is a positive development. Dan, have the interrogations yielded any new insights?"

"That remains unconfirmed as those closest to the matter are sworn to secrecy, under penalty of unlife. What we do know is that our supreme leader has this matter well in hand, um claw, and that all loyal citizens are encouraged to share any information they may have concerning the location of Jett Javelin and or any Fold sympathizers with their local chapter of The Iron."

A loud commotion interrupted the interview and armed Boe warriors rushed into the newsroom and took up positions behind each of the anchors. Jim and Barbara were flummoxed by the uninvited intrusion.

"I see you now have a few new friends of your own," Dan remarked, "welcome to the club. Long live Hazbog!"

"All love Hazbog," the news anchors nervously replied in unison, Jim continued, "Speaking of Fold sympathizers, who all detest, what is being done to root out those traitorous miscreants and round them up?"

"The Iron is generously leading a sweeping effort to uncover all Fold operatives and agents. Our supreme and compassionate leader understands that some citizens may be confused by The Fold's wholesale abandonment of Earth and are possibly unsure of where to place their loyalties. As has been confirmed, The Fold's lies are many and their falsehoods ensure slavery for all of our planet's inhabitants. Those who refuse to be convinced of The Fold's nefarious motives are being introduced to enlightenment camps where they can be shown our glorious new future under The Iron."

"And a glorious future it is," Jim agreed, "In fact, it's been widely reported that the enlightenment camps are outfitted with only the finest amenities so that those being helped there are kept as comfortable as possible. Only a kind and loving leader would take such pains to embrace those who defy him."

"No doubt," Dan continued uneasily, "I visited a camp recently and um, ah, it was, ah, really nice... Hazbog has certainly taken care of everything..."

"We're sure he has. Thanks, Dan. There you have it. Even as Hazbog and his allies heroically dismantle the injustices of The Fold, they are concerned only with their detractors' comfort and wellbeing. That's all for tonight and remember, all love Hazbog!"

The newscast faded and was replaced with a portrait of a fatherly Hazbog embracing several small children. Above the image was a simple slogan *All Love Hazbog, Long Live Hazbog.*

Chapter 33
New Dominion

"Where's Maria?" Jack whispered to Cyd as they were directed down a sterile, institutionally lit concrete block hallway by a group of Boe warriors.

"I think she's still sedated. They're afraid of what she can do to them. Don't want to take any chances, I guess. Can't blame them."

"I guess not. What about us?"

"We're the bait. They don't need her anyhow. Jett's only interested in us anyways."

"Does Hazbog really think Jett's gonna come?"

"Apparently."

"Do you?"

"What do you want me to say?"

"I want you to tell me the truth."

"I've already told you the truth and you've decided not to believe it. But if you want to know, I think one of us is about to be proven right, and it's probably going to be me..."

A gray metal hospital door swung open. Jack and Cyd were roughly shoved through. They were met by the flashing cameras of a media circus. A rowdy press conference was underway with Hazbog presiding at the podium surrounded by

Iron delegates, officers, and Boe henchmen. After a few moments, he motioned in their direction.

"...and here are the perpetrators, these traitors, these agents of The Fold. They are in league with the fugitive Jett Javelin and seek to thrust your world backward into servitude. They conspire to undo all the progress we have made. Remember, it is Jett Javelin's Quantum Swapper that brought The Fold and it's threat of annihilation to Earth and it is he who struck the deal with them to steal your loved ones and imprison them on an icy hell far from home."

Hazbog paused for dramatic effect.

"I stand before you as a liberator and a patriot. Because of my efforts and infinite wisdom, Earth now has a permanent and impenetrable shield surrounding it. I have used The Fold's own neutralization technology against it, and you are safely out of their pernicious grasp. In return, I have asked for only one thing. That thing is Jett Javelin, the Tinker. Yet, it seems that your planet, for all I've sacrificed, has not been able to repay its debt to me. Solarians, I am afraid time is growing short.

"Your inaction has forced upon me a most difficult decision," he apologized, "and left me no choice but to suspend all non-essential services. Food atomizers, water purification systems, and electric power will be discontinued effective immediately. I am certain these *motivators* will incentivize the people of this planet to hasten their search for the Tinker and deliver him to me without delay. Iron forces, with support from my elite Boe warriors, will be stationed at all idled facilities. Anyone caught in violation of this emergency declaration will be charged and sentenced to unlife along with their immediate and extended families. Are there any questions?"

After a few moments of tense silence, a single reporter tentatively raised his hand. Jack shot Cyd an anxious sideways glance.

"Yes, you. What is your question?" Hazbog asked graciously.

The man nervously began, "We are grateful to be liberated from The Fold..."

"Yes, continue."

"As I was saying, we are very grateful, but many people are wondering if Jett Javelin is on this planet or even still alive. There have been no reports of any kind since his alleged disappearance on Alipour several years ago. Jett's own family believes him to be deceased. Despite our best efforts and those of your elite forces, no one has found any trace of him. Don't you feel that this emergency declaration is extreme given the level of cooperation the people of Earth have provided you in your search? All love Hazbog."

"All love Hazbog," the room parroted.

"That is a very interesting question," Hazbog smirked, "My associate here is happy to provide you with the answer you seek," he continued, motioning to a Boe warrior chieftain stationed in front of the podium.

Several Boe descended upon the reporter and dragged him out of the room. This was soon followed by a single agonizing scream and a dull thud. The Boe warriors immediately returned to the press conference without the reporter, glaring at the others menacingly as they retook their places around Hazbog.

Hazbog grinned widely, "Any other questions?"

"Just one," Jack shouted.

"And what is that, traitor?"

"Jack, stop," Cyd pleaded.

"No, Cyd, I need to know. Hazbog, when will you just admit he's dead?"

The crowd gasped and went silent.

"When my hands are the ones that squeeze the light out of him, but first, let's put you on the rack to ensure that happens!"

"He's dead and there's no changing that!" Jack shouted as he was manhandled by two Boe warriors, "you should know better than anyone because you're the one who killed him!"

Before Hazbog could respond, he was distracted by the sound of a ball rolling through the air ducts above them. Everyone did as Hazbog and looked up at the intersecting sheet metal ducting. There was loud bang and the rolling suddenly stopped. This was followed by a commotion inside the vent grate above where Jack and Cyd stood on the raised platform. After a few moments, the vent cover popped off and fell to the floor with a clang. The room stared curiously up into the exposed ducting. Out rolled a single bush bunny. It fell directly into Jack's arms.

"I told you to have this facility fumigated!" Hazbog barked, "I detest those creatures!"

Jack examined the bunny closely, "Nukes? Is that really you girl?"

Nukii purred and cuddled into Jack's bicep.

"It is her!" Cyd cried.

"But she fell into the blood mist with Jett. This isn't possible…"

Rolling momentarily resumed in the duct. Out fell an empty Dr. Pepper can. It landed on the platform and rolled until it was stopped by Hazbog's foot. He crushed it under the heel of his boot.

"Guards!" Hazbog ordered, "Take the fugitives back to their holding cells and set up a perimeter, it appears the Tinker has arrived. Let's do our very best to make him feel welcome," he sneered.

Chapter 34
The Battle for Earth

"Inbound Fold vessel approaching at three quarters light speed," a voice chirped from the navigation console aboard the bridge of Hazbog's vessel.

The Alipouran crew sprang into action.

"Radio Hazbog," the commander ordered, "Radio now!"

Hazbog's grizzled face appeared on a giant monitor that had previous streamed a live image of Solaris 3.

"This is no time for interruption," Hazbog growled, "What is it?"

"All love Hazbog," the commander began.

"Yes, yes, get on with it. The Tinker has tipped his hand and we are tightening the noose. His capture demands my full attention."

"Hazbog, a ship approaches."

"What kind of ship?"

"A Fold ship."

Hazbog's face turned purple and he spat, "Impossible! What are you waiting for? Destroy it!"

"At once, Hazbog."

"Report back to me when this is done," Hazbog's snarling face faded from the screen and was replaced by the Fold craft cruising through space just above Solaris 3's horizon.

"Prepare all weapons. Full assault!" the commander barked, "On my command!"

"Incoming message from Fold vessel," the communications computer announced, "Shall I put it through?"

The commander cocked his head to one side, appearing both surprised and confused at the request, "Yes, put it through."

"Communications link established," the computer relayed and an image of Tii-Eldii surrounded by well-armed Boonan soldiers appeared on the screen.

"Hostile vessel, this is Tii-Eldii of Boona. Our planet owes a great debt to the one called Tinker. We have come to repay that debt. We demand and will accept nothing less than your immediate and unconditional surrender. What say you?"

"No surrender, never! We fight!" the Alipouran commander's battle cry rallied his warriors, "Fire all weapons!"

"Very well, then. You leave us no alternative," Tii-Eldii responded, ending the transmission.

The screen returned to the Fold vessel. The outbound firing of every weapon at the Alipourans' disposal surged toward it. The Boe hooted triumphantly at the ship's imminent demise. Yet just before the energy blasts and munitions reached it, The Fold craft broke up into hundreds of smaller ships that raced off in every direction. Some sped towards the planet's surface while others flanked Hazbog's craft. The assault passed harmlessly through empty space. The Boe's victory hoots and hollers turned to awkward silence. All eyes turned to their commander.

"Alert Hazbog," he ordered, "War we have."

"Tii-Eldii to Boonan teams, commence Operation Liberation. Green, Red, and Blue teams establish a forward operating base west of Hazbog's palace on the planet's surface and begin the ground assault. Orange, Purple, and Versage teams follow my lead. We must take out Hazbog's ship if we are to disable the neutralization field."

The Boonans' small ships gave them a distinct speed and maneuverability advantage and they easily avoided the pulsing weapons of Hazbog's ship, but the armor and energy shields of the single large craft proved problematic for their smaller weapons systems.

"Tii-Eldii, this is Orange 1, their defense systems are rendering our weapons useless. How should we proceed?"

Tii-Eldii's reply was swift, "Engage the munitions swapper. I was hoping to save it but we are left with no alternative."

"Engaging munitions swapper," Orange 1 answered, "Three, two, one... Payload delivered. Delivery confirmed. All squadrons fall back to rendezvous point alpha 7."

"What do you mean 'we have war'?" Hazbog demanded from his chair in the Oval Office, "You have at your disposal the most powerful weapons in this entire sector! You have failed me commander and you will pay dearly for it!"

"I not fail! One ship now many ships, too small to hit!"

"You have failed! Now our entire mission is at risk..."

A flash of light enveloped the ship's bridge and a single metal basket the size of a suitcase appeared on the floor between Hazbog's image and the commander. A white envelope was affixed to it. The commander approached the case with trepidation, plucking off the envelope and opening it. He stared at it intensely for a moment before allowing his arms to go slack. The envelope slipped out of his fingers and wafted slowly to the floor.

"Well... What does it say?" Hazbog sneered.

Before the commander could respond, the basket erupted and the transmission cut out.

"Hazbog, you have to see this!" an Iron operative called from the window.

Hazbog raced across the room, pushing the man to the side and tearing the curtains from the window, he stared up into the sky. The remnants of his command ship rained down into the atmosphere like a fiery meteor storm. Flanking this destruction on all sides were hundreds of Fold craft.

"This is unexpected. The field is still active..." he pondered, before growing angry, "all forces prepare for Fold assault! Show no mercy. Take no prisoners! The battle for Earth has begun. Destroy those craft!"

A barrage of energy beams lit up the sky.

"Hazbog, sir," another Iron operative reported, "there are too many of them! We were not prepared for an invasion from space."

"Silence! I grow weary of excuses! Give them everything we've got! Do not disappoint me..."

As word of The Fold's offensive reached Hazbog's remote outposts, Boe warriors and Iron paramilitary units raced to defend the capital. In the Pacific Northwest where many units were assigned to the ongoing search for Jett, mobilizing quickly proved to be a challenge as most were spread out over large and remote geographic areas.

"Load those hover craft onto the transport now!" an Iron general demanded, "What are you waiting for?"

Several Boe raced to comply with the general's orders, but as they did a large tree trunk smashed into the lead hovercraft and pinned it to the ground. This was followed by a massive rainstorm of trees, rocks, boulders, and miscellaneous debris pummeling them from the sky.

"Take defensive positions! Protect..." the general shouted as he himself was flattened by a large tree trunk.

The relentless attack continued, led by unseen forces lurking just inside the tree line, until every piece of hardware was destroyed or rendered inoperative. Then a blood curdling bellow rose up from the misty forest.

Those who were left unscathed by the initial bombardment tried to flee the area, but they were quickly overrun by a sea of Sasquatch that charged out of the woods. Even the mighty Alipouran warriors were no match for the speed and strength of these creatures and their overwhelming numbers. Soon the entire Iron camp lay in smoldering ruins, littered with the corpses of dead Boe warriors, Iron soldiers, and officers.

Chapter 35
The Battle for Earth Part II

"How could this happen?" Hazbog demanded, "Penetration of a neutralization field is impossible, even for the Aaptuuans. I have been betrayed!"

"Sir, if I may, aren't you the only one who has access to the neutralization field control system?" a nearby colonel asked.

Hazbog's eyes narrowed and his mouth curled up in a menacing grimace. He stomped over to the questioning officer and cocked his head slightly, his clawed hand phasing in and out of existence. He held his claw up and as it phased out, he thrust it into the officer's chest. For a moment, the flummoxed man stared down at Hazbog's nearly invisible forearm. Then it rematerialized, ripping a bloody hole in his ribcage. Eyes wide, the man fell backwards dead, exposing his still beating heart in Hazbog's clutches.

Hazbog casually walked over to another Iron officer, who had been taking notes on a tablet, and smacked squirting organ on its screen, "Anyone else have any traitorous comments?"

Jack stared blankly up at the ceiling of their cell. As far he knew, Maria remained under sedation in the medical wing at the opposite end of the White House complex. Cyd sat on a cot across from him quietly staring at her feet. A slight smirk pulled at the corners of her mouth. Occasionally, Jack would sneak a peek at Nukii, who was being kept in a cage in a nearby cell. Her coos were audible throughout the holding area.

As much as he had refused to acknowledge that Jett may have survived his fall into the blood mist, the mounting evidence that Jett was not only alive but in some altered state of existence here on Earth was overwhelming. He wanted badly to believe his twin brother was still alive, but he was afraid to get his hopes up. There was so much going on right now that was beyond comprehension, he had come to find that approaching new developments with a healthy dose of skepticism was a basic requirement for maintaining one's sanity. Yet, both Nukii and Hazbog, who had succumbed to the same fate on Alipour, were unmistakably alive, so it was not out of the question that Jett may have also survived. Who else would have dropped a Dr. Pepper can from the duct?

"What are you thinking about over there?" Cyd asked.

"What do you think I'm thinking about?"

"That I was right."

"I just can't believe that he might actually..."

"Be alive?" Jett finished his brother's sentence.

Jack and Cyd both leapt up from their cots and spun around toward the voice. Jett stood a few cells away, holding Nukii in one hand and stroking her fur gently with the other. Nukii's audible purring confirmed that this was not an illusion or hologram.

Cyd was the first to speak, "It's about time you showed up! Where have you been? Hazbog is turning Earth upside down looking for you."

"It's nice to see you, too, Cyd. Jack, how are you holding up?"

Jack just stared blankly.

"Okay, I'll come back to you," Jett said, "Cyd, still getting into trouble, I see. How would you both like to get out of there?"

"What do you think?" Cyd smiled, "it's not exactly the Ritz."

Jett, still carrying Nukii, turned semi-transparent and passed through the bars. Nukii fell to the ground with a squeak. She shook herself and rolled between the bars after Jett.

Jett strolled over to their cell and reached his right arm into the digital locking mechanism causing it to explode. The cell door creaked open slowly through the thick acrid smoke. Jett disappeared and Cyd and Jack were once again left alone with Nukii. The entire complex began shaking and dust fell from the ceiling. Muted thuds and booms echoed through the walls.

Tii-Eldii guided his craft through the barrage of energy pulses and surface to air missiles to join his operatives on the front line in a large field on the outskirts of the Washington beltway. Boe warriors and Iron troops had dug into their positions at the east end of the expansive farmland and pummeled the Boonans with shells and kamikaze drones that impacted dramatically against the glowing blue shield that protected the landing site.

Tii-Eldii gathered his captains around him as incessant explosions impacted the shield's surface above them.

"Intelligence from our orbiting units confirms that the neutralization field remains active despite the destruction of the mother ship. We now believe the trigger must be here on the planet's surface and most probably in the possession of Hazbog himself who we know to be holed up in what is known as The White House. We also know that at a large contingent of Hazbog's Boe warriors were onboard the ship when it was destroyed," Tii-Eldii continued, "leaving them in a largely scattered and unprepared defensive posture with little to no reinforcement capability. The only thing standing between us and Hazbog are the troops stationed at the opposite end of this battlefield."

"Tii-Eldii, we have also suffered heavy losses between the asteroid belt and the initial landing maneuvers. Even with our early victory against his mothership, Hazbog's forces have us outnumbered on the ground and if we don't act quickly, we will be outflanked. Reports coming in from the front state that significant reinforcements are mobilizing in the western portions of this continent and are currently en route."

"We knew well before we arrived that this would be a difficult endeavor and that many of our brethren would be lost. But we came anyway because of our honor and the debt we owe to the citizens of this planet. We will fight to the last. We will fight to the finish! For Boona!"

"For Boona!" the officers shouted in unison.

"Now, advance the shield. Move all units to the front. We will wait until we are upon them, then we will open the shield and overrun their positions. We have units on the ground and in the airspace above the city. We must apprehend or eliminate Hazbog by sundown. For honor!"

"For honor!" they responded and bellowed a battle cry that sent shivers down the spines of every Iron soldier waiting on the receiving end of their onslaught.

"Where the hell did he go?" Jack exclaimed, "I'm really confused right now..."

Cyd poked her head out into the empty hallway, "All of the guards are gone. Let's find Maria."

"I wonder where they all went."

"Who cares. Let's get out of here."

The booming and shaking continued to grow louder and harder as dust and tiles fell from the ceiling. The lights flickered on and off. Nukii growled at the commotion.

"It's okay, girl. We're just gonna find our friend," Jack whispered down to this bush bunny who was certainly real enough to convince him that the apparition he had seen a few moments before was his brother and not a ghost or illusion.

Jack ran behind Cyd as she hurried down one debris ridden hallway after another.

"Cyd, where are we going?"

"Just listen."

Though it was difficult to hear over the booming thuds and violent shaking, Jack could make out a soft, yet distant voice every time they came to a juncture. The voice simply said, "This way" and Cyd would turn in that direction.

"Is that my brother?"

"I hope so."

The deserted passageways were both welcome and unexpectedly unnerving as they would normally be filled with Hazbog's henchmen. Whatever was going on outside required the full attention of everyone at Hazbog's disposal. After a few more twists and turns, Jack and Cyd arrived at a door plainly labeled *Infirmary.* Cyd gently turned the knob and the door opened. There, in a hospital bed surrounded by beeping monitors, lay Maria. Jett stood next to her. Nukii purred wildly.

Jett said, "I'm glad you're both here. Let's wake your friend up so we can finish this."

Jack tried to speak, but once again couldn't find any words. Cyd ran over to Jett.

"I knew you were still alive. I never doubted it for a minute! Though there was no convincing your brother," she paused, "Jett, there's something, I don't know... different about you."

Jett looked at Cyd with deep sad eyes, eyes that had seen too much, and replied, "Have you ever watched your own funeral? Have you ever just looked on helplessly as everyone you ever loved mourned your death? Have you ever wanted so badly to tell them all you're okay, but couldn't because if you revealed yourself it would put them all in mortal danger? I've been with you guys this whole time. I just couldn't let you know. Hazbog would've detected my physical manifestation immediately, yet no matter how careful I was, he was always one step behind me."

Jack finally mustered up the resolve to ask, "Physical manifestation, what does that mean?"

"As Cyd noticed, I am not like you anymore. Not human, anyway. As my quantum sickness worsened, the suit became useless and I was no longer able to maintain my physical form for more than a few minutes. At this moment, the pain of being here with you is beyond description," he grimaced, "We don't have much time. I created this mess and now I have to make it right."

Jett held his hands over Maria's forehead and what looked like glowing bits of snow descended from his palms and disappeared into her temples only to reappear moments later as translucent streams dripping from her fingertips. Maria sat up with a start.

"Where am I?"

Cyd grabbed her by her shoulders and said, "Are you able to stand? We have to get out of here! Jett, what's the quickest way out?"

"He's gone," Jack said, "again..."

"Look here," Cyd pointed.

Burned into the floor at the foot of the bed were four simple words - *Find the blue light.*

Chapter 36
Desperate Times

Hazbog stood alone, hunched before a wall of monitors that streamed various angels of the battle raging outside. The Boonans' blue forcefield dome advanced rapidly on his last lines of defense and his decimated forces prepared to make their final stand. With his mother ship destroyed and his troops scattered across the planet, his options were quickly narrowing. If his luck didn't change quickly, The Fold would soon have him sequestered again in Tower 100.

"Not going quite the way you expected?" a familiar voice said.

Hazbog spun around angrily. Jett was seated comfortably at the head of the long mahogany conference table with his hands resting on his belly.

"You…"

"Why so surprised? You've been tearing this planet up looking for me. Well… here I am. It's your move."

"You dare speak to me in such a way! I should have killed you on Alipour when I had the chance!"

"Don't beat yourself up. You gave it your best shot when you threw me into the blood mist. I'm surprised it didn't work."

"I wasn't trying to kill you. I just wanted everyone to believe you were dead."

"Why is that?"

"Isn't it obvious?"

"Afraid not. Enlighten me."

"You are The Fold's pet project and your planet is one of its riskiest experiments. To turn you and Solaris 3 against them would be my way of thanking them for 3,500 years of imprisonment and their complete annihilation of my civilization. I would love nothing more than to spoil the whole thing for them."

"But that can't be your only reason."

"No, it is not. I am quite interested in your quantum suit."

"Discovered quantum sickness, have you?" Jett smiled, "take it from me, it's a bitch, and it gets much, much worse. The suit is only a band-aid. It slows the sickness down, but it doesn't cure it or reverse the condition. As you can see, I don't wear it anymore. I left it on a faraway world in a time long forgotten. To survive, I received help from other, um travelers, but that help comes at a very steep price. Hazbog, you have no idea the suffering that awaits you."

Hazbog seethed, "I can handle any suffering, boy! You and your planet are the ones who will suffer now!"

Jett smiled, "Where do you think I've been these last few years while you searched the galaxy for me? What do you believe happened after the blood mist?"

"I believe I miscalculated the quantum swap and you were mistakenly sent somewhere other than where I intended," Hazbog spat.

"Well, if that's legitimately what you think, you're naiver than I thought. I wonder, has Ripeem visited you much lately?"

"What do you know of Ripeem?"

Jett smirked and with a quick wave goodbye, vanished.

"We wouldn't want to give too much away," Ripeem's voice casually interrupted, "now would we?"

Jack, Cyd, Maria, and Nukii emerged from a hatch hidden in the lawn of the Rose Garden. The sky above them was filled with smoke and deafening explosions shook the ground beneath their feet. In the distance above the city skyline, a large blue dome of light approached. Nukii began munching on the lush rose bushes.

"Thank God for exit signs," Cyd shouted above the commotion, "What now?"

Maria pointed to the blue dome, "We need to go there!"

"Why? What's over there?" Jack asked.

"That's the blue light!"

"You want to go toward the battle? Are you crazy? Cyd?"

"I don't see any other blue lights, do you?"

Jack became agitated, "If we go over there, we're going to get killed or captured."

"That's what Jett wants us to do. Why else would he write that on the floor?"

A bolt of blue energy shot up from the dome in a long arc and hit the White House, blowing the West Wing to pieces. Shrapnel rained down all around them.

"Run!" Maria screamed as another bolt arced their way and exploded on the lawn behind them.

Jack scooped up Nukii and the three scurried away from the onslaught of energy beams that vaporized The White House piece by piece and ran toward the blue dome. Fleeing Iron soldiers and Boe warriors raced past in the opposite direction, and took little interest in them, as the blue light engulfed their defensive positions and myriad blue rays eviscerated their fortifications.

"Are you sure this is a good idea?" Jack shouted, but his voice was drowned out by the cacophony of war, and they hurried on past the smoking ruins of once stately city blocks formerly occupied by the world's powerful and elite.

Soon they arrived at the edge of the giant blue energy dome. Inside it were large tentacled alien creatures rushing forward, mercilessly slaying every enemy soldier they confronted. One of the creatures looked up from the melee and locked eyes with Jack. It held one of its clawed tentacles up in a way that caused the rest to stop in their tracks. Boe warriors and Iron soldiers used the pause in the Boonan offensive as an opportunity to escape the onslaught and scattered in every direction.

Cyd turned to Jack, "I think that one has its eyes on you. All eight of them."

Jack didn't respond. He appeared to be in a trance and stood perfectly still with a blank stare pasted across his face. Except for the one who locked eyes with Jack, the rest of the creatures dropped to a knee and bowed their heads. A low hum that resembled a religious chant rose up from the battlefield. The leader slowly approached Jack, never breaking eye contact or acknowledging either Cyd or Maria's presence. Nukii chirped and popped out of Jack's frozen arms. She rolled vigorously toward the creature and stopped at its feet. Without breaking its stare, the creature picked Nukii up and swaddled her in its tentacles.

"I think Nukii knows that thing," Cyd marveled, remembering the stories Jett had told her about his time on Lanedaar 3, "Tii-Eldii?"

"Who's Tii-Eldii?" Maria asked.

But before Cyd could answer her, the creature lifted its clawed tentacle and placed it on Jack's forehead. Jack began to speak.

"I am Tii-Eldii," Jack said through his trance, "And you are the sibling of the great Jett Javelin. I have come with my brothers from Boona to liberate your people from the menace known as Hazbog. Once we have done this, we will have repaid our debt to Jett and the people of Solaris 3. Lead us to Hazbog and to victory!"

Tii-Eldii removed his claw from Jack's head and Jack stumbled backwards, slowly regaining consciousness.

"You're Tii-Eldii?"

The creature simply nodded and pointed in the direction of The White House.

"That's right," Cyd pointed, "Hazbog is in there."

Tii-Eldii raised his clawed tentacle and thrust it toward Hazbog's layer. The Boonans' roared a blood curdling battle cry as they leapt to their feet in unison and charged toward the flaming wreckage that was once The White House. Tii-Eldii handed Nukii back to Jack and with a wave invited the three of them to join the fight.

Chapter 37
Desperate Measures

The underground bunker shook violently. Books flew off shelves, lights flickered erratically, and monitor turned one by one to static as their camera feeds went offline. Hazbog cursed as he paced the room, pieces and parts of his body phasing in and out.

"Give too much of what away? Do you take me for a fool?"

"I do and you've proven me right time and again," Ripeem chuckled, "do you take me for an Eelshakian Admiral?"

"I never have," Hazbog admitted, "I am not sure what you are, but you are much more than any Admiral I've ever known."

"If you knew I was something other than that which I appeared, why did you continue to play along? Wait, don't answer. I already know the reason. It would have been unwise for you to question my motives as you have only a single motivation, yourself. You foolishly believe the quantum suit will save your sorry hide, but you are wrong. The Fold possesses no such technology."

"It worked for the Tinker, at least for a short while."

"It only *appeared* to work."

"I don't understand."

"That's always been a challenge for you..."

"You told me the suit would fix my condition! The Tinker was never your goal, you are working at cross purposes. You lied to me!"

"You lied to yourself, Hazbog, but those lies have served me well."

The Boonan troops advanced quickly on the smoldering ruins of The White House in the wake of the fleeing Iron and Boe forces. Energy cages filled to capacity with captured enemy combatants. All that remained was the apprehension of Hazbog himself and the acquisition of his neutralization field controller. They were both housed together deep beneath the now leveled White House complex.

At Tii-Eldii's behest, Jack, Cyd, and Maria stayed with him toward the rear of the advancing Boonan front. Once they arrived back on the charred lawn, Jack searched about the rose garden for the secret hatch from which the three had recently emerged. He grabbed one of Tii-Eldii's tentacles and pointed toward it. Tii-Eldii placed his claw on Jack's forehead for a moment and then nodded knowingly.

"What did you say?" Cyd asked.

"I told him about the hatch and the secret tunnels where Hazbog may still be hiding. His troops are setting up a perimeter and as soon as they do, we will head in there with Tii-Eldii and lead the Boonans straight to Hazbog."

"How do you know where Hazbog is?" Maria asked.

"I don't, but I have a feeling that Jett does, and just as he led us to Tii-Eldii, he may do the same with Hazbog."

"How can you be sure?"

"Do you have a better idea?"

"How about we let Tii-Eldii and his friends go in there without us. We'll just slow them down," Maria argued.

Jack frowned, "not going to happen. I want to see that bastard taken down. I want to see the look on his ugly face."

"And risk getting killed?" Maria challenged.

"I'm pretty sure that's all I've been doing since I hooked up with the two of you. Plus, what are you worried about? You should be the least concerned of any of us."

"That's fair," Cyd agreed.

"Only," Maria started, "never mind..."

With the perimeter now in place, Tii-Eldii signaled the three of them to follow him to the hatch. He barked orders in Boonan to his soldiers, a dozen or so of which charged into the tunnel to root out any remaining resistance. Tii-Eldii then waved Jack, Cyd, and Maria into the dim tunnel, quickly following them. With the bombardment halted, the tunnel, littered with debris and filled with settling dust, was eerily quiet. The Boonan soldiers lined up against the wall and awaited further orders. Tii-Eldii looked at Jack and the girls.

Cyd said, "I think they're waiting for us to tell them which way to go."

Jack listened intently, hoping that his brother would provide guidance, but there was nothing, not a sign or a clue anywhere.

"Well?" Maria asked, "Any word from Jett?"

"Not yet, but I think I remember how to get back to our holding cells. They were pretty close to Hazbog's bunker. Cyd and I could hear him yelling through the walls."

"Yeah, he wasn't too far from us," Cyd agreed, "Lead the way."

Jack waved his arm to Tii-Eldii and made his way into the tunnel, but Tii-Eldii grabbed him by the shoulder, holding him back for moment. Tii-Eldii nodded to a couple of his soldiers to walk in front of Jack. Following Jack's instructions, they cautiously crept toward the cell block, but they didn't make it far before the tunnel was rocked by a powerful explosion. Clouds of dust billowed down on them along with pieces of the ceiling and broken glass from the fluorescent tube lights. Several sections of the roof caved in, separating Tii-Eldii and Cyd from Jack, Nukii, and Maria, and the Boonan soldiers at the front.

"Cyd! Cyd! Are you okay?" Jack called as he helped Maria up from the floor.

"Yes," came a muffled reply, "I'm with Tii-Eldii, but he's hurt and he's not moving," she cried, "What do I do?"

Maria balanced herself. She stepped up to the pile of rocks and concrete, "Don't worry, Cyd," she called, "we're coming," she said, instinctively raising her hands to move the debris out of their way, but her energy reflected back and forth within a narrow bubble surrounding her. Maria tried a second time with no luck. A third try proved no better.

Maria stared perplexed at her hands, "I don't understand..."

"I'm afraid you've be neutralized," a voice said, "Hazbog saw to that."

Nukii growled. Maria and Jack spun around. Standing in the hallway behind them was the old fisherman.

"It's you!" Maria gasped.

"You know him?"

"Yes, he took care of me after my parents..."

"I thought the Big Foot did that."

"Not entirely... I would've died if not for him," she stared at him, "You disappeared years ago. I thought you were dead. How are you here right now?"

The old fisherman's mouth turned up in a playful grin, "I'm not. I never was."

Chapter 38
Traveler's Travails

"Tii-Eldii? Tii-Eldii?" Cyd prodded the large Boonan with her foot, "Tii-Eldii c'mon, wake up..."

Tii-Eldii groaned loudly and Cyd jumped back. Despite visiting several planets and interacting with many aliens, being trapped alone with a creature of this size in a dark tunnel left Cyd feeling skittish and uneasy. She knew rationally that she had nothing to fear as Jett had regaled her with many Tii-Eldii tales during their early friendship, but no matter, she couldn't help the way she felt.

She attempted to rouse him again, "Tii-Eldii?" but it was no use, so she called out to Jack and Maria who she assumed were still on the other side of the debris pile, "Maria? Jack? Can you guys hear me?"

No response came and her voice simply echoed back in her ears.

"Be calm my child," a voice reassured.

Cyd spun around and there stood Brother Duc wearing a brown frock, casually leaning against the wall.

"How did you know where to find us?"

"I've been with you all along, my dear, Abcde."

"What do you mean you *never was*?" Maria asked the old fisherman.

"Just as I'm not here now."

"What is he talking about, Maria?"

"I have no idea."

"I am everywhere and nowhere. I am young, old, alive, and dead. I am as all things are, infinite."

"What do you want from me? Why did you help me?"

"Maria, I knew if I allowed those Solarian hacks to continue to experiment on you, they would have eventually created more creatures like you, more deviations to the natural order of things."

"I don't understand."

"You don't realize it, but you and your friend Acbde were genetically engineered using a cocktail of alien DNA cooked up by The Fold's best and brightest. That is why you are both so unique. Their goal is that if one day the Aaptuuans were to disappear, humanity might act as a replacement. But you and your planet are not special, they are interfering with the evolution of many potential successor races."

"You mean The Fold made me this way?"

"Yes. You and you friend are both victims of their overreach, as is your entire planet. I protected you from them when you were a child and I will continue to do so now. Unfortunately, your protection requires the temporary suspension of your special abilities, which Hazbog has so kindly assisted me with. For this final leg of your journey, there will be no more magic tricks."

"What's your game?" Jack demanded.

"Sadly, young Jack, even if I told you, you would never remember."

"Wake up, my friend."

Tii-Eldii struggled to open his eyes. A blurry Boonan form stood above him in the tunnel.

"What happened?"

"The tunnel collapsed, but thankfully no one was hurt," the voice continued, extending a hand to lift Tii-Eldii from the floor.

Tii-Eldii held his aching head and tried to steady his vision. After a few moments, the form came into focus.

"Ripeem? Is it really you?"

"It's as much me as it's ever been."

"I don't understand. You died repairing the ark... That was over a hundred years ago," Tii-Eldii groaned.

"Ahhh, yes, one of my very favorite stunts. I was convincing, yes?"

Tii-Eldii was stunned.

"I'll take that as a yes. Sorry about the whole neutralization thing, but I was curious to see how quickly The Fold would react to the hyper-lightspeed testing. I have to admit, they were right on top of it. Nice job with the arks, though. In all the time I've observed The Fold's playthings, I've never witnessed something as creative as that."

"Who are you?"

"Just a weary traveler coming to the end of my own very long road."

Cyd heard scratching and crunching coming from the other side of the debris pile and momentarily turned away from Brother Duc. Pebbles rolled down the pile. Cyd ran over and began digging in earnest. Soon, the tunnel opened up and Boonan warriors flooded in. When she looked back, Brother Duc was gone.

Tii-Eldii still lay unconscious on the ground. Several Boonans rushed to his aid while the others began digging through the debris to where Jack and Maria were trapped. One, who must have been a medic, removed a blue cylinder from his belt and gave Tii-Eldii a shot in the tentacle. Tii-Eldii gasped and sat straight up.

"Traveler!"

Cyd raised his claw to her forehead, "You must have been dreaming," she thought.

"Ripeem was there," he panted, "He was there!"

Tii-Eldii painfully rose to his feet and stumbled unsteadily over to his men who had managed to dig through to the other side. Cyd ran in front of them and through the opening.

"Maria! Jack! Are you guys okay?"

Cyd looked desperately in every direction, but there was no sign of her friends. They were gone.

"Maybe they went back outside," she theorized, but with the extent of the cave-in, the only exit was the one they had just come through.

Tii-Eldii placed his claw on Cyd's forehead, "I believe Hazbog is not the greatest evil we are facing. Something far more sinister is lurking in these tunnels…"

Chapter 39
Sum of it All

Hazbog said nothing to Jack and Maria as he anxiously tapped a single claw on the mahogany table in an erratic rhythm. He sat at its head, in President Montoya's chair, staring at his other hand with a perplexed expression as it silently phased in and out of reality. Jack and Maria sat opposite him and occasionally shared a glance as guards stood menacingly on either side of their brown leather chairs. Other than the five of them, the large room was vacant. At long last Hazbog lifted his eyes from the nearly invisible appendage.

"I don't know what's worse, falling apart mentally in Tower 100 or physically on your planet," his voice echoed in the empty chamber, "the two of you will be confronted with this question soon enough. Once the Aaptuuan pawns have succeeded in overrunning my forces, there's an excellent chance you'll both end up back in Tower 100, but for me, I will choose an honorable death. I will not be made their slave again," Hazbog paused for a moment and with a wide grin continued, "but what will you do?"

"I'm not sure what you mean," Jack replied, "Why would they do anything to us? You're the one they have a problem with."

"I spent 3,542 years fixing things that otherwise could fix themselves without my help. I've lived far too many lifetimes for any creature. What was their purpose other than to keep me as a curiosity? As a demonstration of their dominion? To humiliate me... I am no better for their *mentoring...*"

"So, what, then, you decide to take it out on us? We didn't have anything to do with it," Jack spat, "and by the way, how's attacking our planet working out for you?"

"The Fold destroyed my entire system! For what? Yet they give Solaris chance upon chance. You are not so different from me. You are barbaric and bloodthirsty! You place your own priorities above those of all other creatures on your planet. You kill each other with reckless abandon and turn your planet to ash as the great sedated masses look on as if this were the natural order of things. You are no better than Eelshak! So *why* are you spared!?"

Jack and Maria were silent. Nukii growled.

"Well, what do you have to say for yourselves?" Hazbog howled, "Even when you are presented with paradise, you can't help yourselves. You respond by creating The Iron and laying out the welcome mat for me. It's unfathomable," he snortled, "You see, it's precisely what I would do. You have no idea how I burned to revolt against them in Tower 100, but I have to admit, this is a lot more fun, even it is my last hoorah."

Finally, Maria spoke up, "You're right. Why should The Fold decide who lives and who dies?"

"Are you serious? He's a psychopath! Why are you agreeing with him?"

"You are both correct," a familiar voice interrupted, "The Fold should not decide and this creature is truly a psychopath."

"You snake! You liar! How dare you come back here!" Hazbog bellowed.

"Come back? I never left. I never have. I never will, not even in death. I've been here all along. I'm everywhere. The Fold knows me as the Traveler, and I'll have you know; I've been to Eelshak many times. I first went there long before you were born. Horrifically fascinating place. One of most brutal societies ever spawned. Who do you think detonated the black hole generator on your home planet just before The Fold could neutralize your system? You would have done it yourselves eventually, I simply helped things along. In the end, I did the universe a huge favor by removing that cesspool from its midst.

"And let me tell you, The Fold never witnessed anything like that. A black hole generator! Quite clever of your species to come up with it. Truly astounding! Imagine my surprise when the contraption actually worked. I'm shocked The Fold decided to save your sorry hide from the frozen oblivion of space with the misplaced belief they could rehabilitate you. You should be grateful, but instead you've decided to clutch on to your hate and rage all these long years. I suppose it's not your fault, it's your nature."

Hazbog shot up out of his chair, seething.

"Come now, Hazbog. Can't you see it now? It me who arranged for you to meet the Tinker and later fix his brother's plumbing, which I *coincidentally* broke. I'm the one who granted you access to the Quantum Swapper and the one that inspired Jett to create it in the first place. You know, it's the little things. Everyone is so focused on the big things, the *notable events*, that they miss the myriad little things that lead them to wherever they happen to find themselves at any particular moment in time," the Traveler turned to Jack, "most recently I was Brother Duc, Winchester Willie, and the beguiling old fisherman. You have all been unwitting pawns in a great game you are only now just beginning to grasp. But don't feel badly, for your participation serves a higher purpose. Even The Fold is unaware aware of my intentions," he concluded.

"This is all your fault? You made Jett make the swapper?"

"Why don't you ask him?"

Jett appeared seated at the table across from Jack.

"Ask me what?"

Hazbog's jaw fell slack, *"You had him this whole time? You've played me for a fool!"*

"Pipe down, Hazbog," the Traveler responded, "we have bigger issues to work through than your bruised ego. Jett, your brother would like to know whose fault all of this truly is."

Jett turned to his brother and said simply, "The Fold's."

"What are you talking about? The Fold saved your life. They made you the quantum suit."

"I wouldn't have needed the suit if they hadn't taken Dad to Pluto."

"But you're the one who made that deal with them, I mean, to take all the murderers."

"Don't you get it? I was trying to save our planet from me, from my invention. I was fourteen years old. What did I know? Neither one of us knew what Dad had done in Iraq. I thought I was doing the right thing. The Aaptuuans knew what the consequences would be and let me make the deal anyway."

Jack pointed to the Traveler, "But *he* started all of this. He said he gave you the idea for the Quantum Swapper. He created this mess! Now look at you. You're some kind of ghost."

"If you truly understood what The Fold is and who is really calling the shots, you would understand that the Aaptuuans are pawns, too, and that we are their pawns, the pawns of pawns."

"I am no pawn!" Hazbog barked.

"You are the biggest fool of all if that's what you believe," Jett argued, "Ever since the bloodmist on Alipour, you have turned the galaxy upside down looking for me. I'm sure you wondered why I didn't arrive on the other side of the swap as you expected."

"Of course I did," Hazbog hissed, "but I surmised it was a malfunction in your machine or caused by your quantum suit. It's obvious to me now that this Traveler stole you from me. This whole thing is outrageous!"

"Not the whole thing," the Traveler interrupted, "Remember, Hazbog, it's the little things. The smallest things make the universe go 'round, and you, my friend, are a very small thing. Now, Hazbog, I now require you to make a small decision."

Hazbog raised a brow, "What would that be?"

"Will you return to Tower 100 or, do as you previously declared..." the traveler challenged.

A beautifully gilded samurai sword appeared on the table in front of Hazbog, "See you on the other side," the Traveler grinned before a flash left Hazbog alone in the room with the gleaming sword and his two Boe guards.

The pounding of heavy footsteps and shouts from Boonan soldiers rose up just outside the heavily fortified door. The door frame became outlined by a bright red light and, after a moment, it fell inward to the floor with a clang. Boonan warriors stormed into room and quickly subdued the guards. Hazbog stared down at the sword.

"It's over, Hazbog," Cyd declared, "Tell us where Maria and Jack are!"

"I wouldn't think of it!" Hazbog laughed maniacally, "For Eelshak!" he cried out, turning the sword on himself and plunging it into his heart.

Chapter 40
A Grand Compromise

Dr. VaaCaam-a stood in front of a large window that looked out across the surface of Solaris 9 and into the infinite expanse of space beyond. The rehabilitation domes that had once held millions of Solarian abductees slowly rose up from the surface and left the dwarf planet in an orderly fashion. Tii-Eldii, who was seated next to Jett, bowed his head silently while he gently stroked Nukii's fur. Jack nervously examined the large aqueous tanks that held Cyd and Maria in a state of suspended animation. Le-Wa and Chi-Col silently flanked their leader.

VaaCaam-a slowly pivoted to face those present and announced, "With Hazbog gone and the Neutralization Field deactivated, we have decided that it is time to end this phase of our mission and return the rehabilitated to Solaris 3," he paused, then his tone became grave, "but that is not the only phase that must conclude," he continued, "the being that brought you here is known to us only as The Traveler. We have observed its involvement in many chaotic events throughout galactic history. While we understand little of The Traveler's origins, we believe that its motivations lie in direct contrast to our own."

"You are very astute, VaaCaam-a," The Traveler's disembodied voice agreed.

"Welcome, Traveler," VaaCaam-a said, "We have been eagerly awaiting your arrival. What brings you to the Solaris system?"

"I am tempted to ask you the same question, but I already know the answer."

"Do you?"

"Yes, it is quite obvious you are grooming many civilizations, including this one, as potential replacements to your own. The poor souls of this system are yet the latest victims of your ceaseless meddling. They deserve to seek a fate of their own rather than have it dictated by you and your ilk."

"And why are you so certain this primitive and barbaric species would make a suitable replacement?"

"I never said it would. In fact, it probably wouldn't. We can all agree that with their current state of affairs, they will most likely destroy themselves and their planet. Yet, with some genetic manipulation and societal grooming, the outcome could be carefully crafted to take whatever form The Fold chooses. With enough time and pressure any lump of coal can be turned to a sparkling diamond, albeit an artificial one."

Jack looked at Le-Wa and Chi-Col in disbelief, "is this true?"

They looked at each other for a moment and reluctantly nodded.

"Was my people's suffering also justified by this very same goal?" Tii-Eldii demanded.

"Each race is evaluated independently without prejudice," VaaCaam-a responded, "we have no motive above that of keeping peace."

"You are liars," The Traveler accused, "and you violate your own laws, which also makes you hypocrites. Here you exploit the Boonans' obligation to the Tinker as an excuse to murder the Boe and their allies by proxy. You are corrupt. Your enforcement of the Ten Laws often requires you to violate the very laws you espouse and hold others accountable to, but where is your accountability?"

"We are accountable only to The Great White Light."

"A being whose own motivations you proclaim to understand, but obviously do not."

"And what do you know of The Great White Light?"

"I only know that your blind faith in its presumed ideology has led you to murder countless trillions in the name of peace, love, and order."

"We seek only to protect the innocent from the expansionist conquests of the violent."

"But you only concern yourselves with the violent when their technology begins to rival your own. Who, may I ask, are you really protecting? If you are as principled as you proclaim to be, why would you sit idly by as a witness to depravity and murder so long as it is contained within your own artificial parameters?"

Jett interjected, "You've watched our planet for thousands of years and allowed wars, genocide, and disease to ravage it. Where were you during the Holocaust, the bombing of Hiroshima, the Black Plague, 9/11, the Spanish Inquisition, the European conquest of the Americas, and millions of other dark events? You allowed them to occur because they didn't threaten The Fold. Not until my swapper came along did you determine it was time to intervene on Solaris 3."

"I know that all of this is difficult for you to understand, Jett," VaaCaam-a replied, "but..."

"But nothing," Jett continued, "The Traveler has revealed to me all of your various 'good' deeds and I have to vehemently disagree. I understand all too well the peace you're trying to keep."

"Jett, Earth is peaceful now. Everyone has everything they need. The Fold has brought an end to the suffering and the inequality," Jack argued.

Jett stared his brother down, "and in exchange Earth gave up its freedom and innovation and culture. Was that the best thing for us to do? Is comfort worth abandoning liberty? Are we really ready for this? What if The Iron is our way of fighting for what makes us human in the first place? The Fold wants to turn us into them, but we are not them. We may never be, and what then? Lights out?"

"Your planet has made tremendous progress in such a short time. It would be tragic to reverse course now. Is it your desire to return things to the way they were before the Quantum Swapper? I need not remind you of the self-destructive path your species was on prior to our timely intervention."

"No, you don't, but it was our path..."

"Jett, you don't understand what you're saying," Jack interrupted, "what has The Traveler done to you? I feel like I don't know you anymore."

"That's because I'm no longer the person you knew. I'm not even human anymore," Jett held up his arm and phased it in and out of existence, "if not for The Traveler, I wouldn't be anything anymore. If you want to know what's in store for you, Jack, take a close look at our friends," he nodded toward Cyd and Maria.

The Traveler's voice agreed, "These females are a perfect example of The Fold's intentions. Both are products of Aaptuuan genetic engineering that has been taking place on Solaris 3 for millennia. What the Aaptuuans have not told you is that by slowly introducing select alien genome into yours, they have potentially created a hybrid that is greater than the sum of its parts. So, you see, they are not just changing your society, they are changing you - who and what you are is slowly being replaced by their vision of who and what they believe you should be."

"We only do this out of kindness and love. Without our oversight, humanity would still be mired in darkness."

"You do not know this for certain," The Traveler argued.

"We have sufficient statistical evidence collected across millions of systems to reinforce our position in this matter. We do not and have never acted recklessly. In each individual case, we seek only to improve the outcome for those we guide on their path to enlightenment."

"And yet, you never ask if they seek enlightenment…"

Tii-Eldii, who was becoming increasingly agitated, cut The Traveler off, "When the Great Darkness beset my system, we had begun to make significant strides toward the kind of peace and equality espoused by The Ten Laws. No, we were not perfect, and abuses still existed, but we made steady progress, nonetheless. We did not do this because we feared the wrath of some higher power, but because it made sense for our people and our civilization. Would it have been better for us to arrive at this conclusion ourselves or to have been coerced by fear of retribution? For my people, retribution came anyway, because although we were making progress, that progress did not occur at a pace that placated The Fold. My people paid dearly, and I suffered a hundred years of solitude as a consequence of slower pacing. How is this fair? How is this equitable? How is this just?"

"The enforcement of The Ten Laws is often accompanied by sacrifice and difficulty. We are not ignorant to the controversial methods employed in bringing offending systems into compliance, but neutralization is preferable to obliteration. You would have to agree with this perspective."

Jett spat, "That's like arguing that slavery is better than genocide. They are both terrible. The lesser of two evils is still evil."

"What do you want then?" VaaCaam-a asked.

"A test," The Traveler's voice suggested, "and a truce."

"What are you inferring?" VaaCaam-a responded.

"A fresh start for Earth, for things to return to the way they were before I invented the swapper," Jett said.

"That would be quite impossible," VaaCaam-a pointed out.

"Quite impossible for you, maybe," The Traveler said, "but I'm all about impossible. However, the reset, like a neutralization, will not be without sacrifice."

"If you can reset everything back to the way it was before, then what is the sacrifice?" Jack asked.

"A reset is not a rewind, Jack. If The Fold agrees, we can make it appear as though there was never a swapper, a rehabilitation program, or any extraterrestrial interference at all. However, time will still have passed. Young children will have grown and we cannot resurrect the dead. What we can do is replace memories of what occurred with a *modified* narrative."

"And what about the moon? If you remember, thanks to Hazbog, there's a huge chunk of it missing."

"Jack, so far as your people will be concerned, the moon will have always been that way," The Traveler answered.

"You argue that we defy The Ten Laws and now you implore us to rewrite the history of an entire world? What you are suggesting is mass amnesia for billions of Solarians, and what will you replace the last several years of their memories with? What fiction will you craft?"

"Only what is necessary to undo what you've done."

"And if The Fold agrees to your proposal, what benefit would there be for us?"

"That is the truce. If you indulge me by allowing Solaris 3 to evolve outside of your influence, as an experiment of sorts, I will not interfere with your efforts elsewhere."

"And what is the proposed the length of your truce?"

"Assuming that you leave the Solaris system alone, can we agree to a term of one thousand Solarian years?"

"Please allow me to confer with my associates," VaaCaam-a said.

"Oh, and one more thing," the Traveler's voice continued, "you must take the two female mutants with you. They are corrupted and cannot remain on Solaris 3."

A long silence ensued as the three Aaptuuans telepathically debating the merits of The Traveler's proposal. Jack squirmed uncomfortably in his chair while Jett stared at him with a look in his eyes that communicated he already knew what the outcome would be.

During the long Aaptuuan conference, Jett smiled at Tii-Eldii and said, "you were a very good friend to me, the best a boy could ask for. Please consider your debt to Solaris repaid, and let your people know of my undying gratitude for their great sacrifice."

"Thank you, Jett. Consider it done," Tii-Eldii smiled.

Jett smiled in return and brought his attention back to Jack, whose eyes continued to dart about the room.

VaaCaam-a eventually nodded to Le-Wa and Chi-Col and then addressed the room, "Before we share our decision, which has been ratified by the High Council of Aaptuu 4, I first want to address the tinker directly. Jett, it saddens us that you have made this reckless request for yourself and your planet. We do not understand what we have done to turn you against us so that you would become aligned with this being, but our hand has been forced and the decision that has been made, has been made with the balance of the galaxy in mind. We are prepared to sacrifice the wellbeing of Solaris 3 and leave it to its own fate, but Jett you must understand, that due to your condition, you will never be able to return to your previous life. If we go through with your desired course of action, all memory of you will be wiped from Solarian history and from the minds of those who knew you."

Jett looked at VaaCaam-a and said, "I accept this. It is a small price to pay for my planet's freedom."

"So be it. The Fold accepts The Traveler's terms and will begin an immediate withdrawal from the Solaris system."

"What do you mean there'll be no memory of Jett? You're my brother. I won't forget you!"

The Traveler calmly said, "Jack, your memories are not your own, they flow from the universe, and I will divert that flow ever so slightly, so that you will not miss your brother. He may, however, miss you."

"Don't worry, I'll keep an eye on you, Jack." Jett smiled, ran his hand through his blue hair, and vanished.

Nukii squealed.

"And so, it is agreed and so it is sealed," The Traveler's voice echoed and faded out.

All in the room vanished as the last of the domes departed Solaris 9.

Chapter 42
...and The Fold

Jack looked up at the clock.

"Two-thirty," he moaned. Another half-hour before he could go home and play some pickup street hockey with his friends.

"Mr. Javelin, is there something you'd like to share with the rest of the class?" Mrs. Aspen asked.

"Huh?" Jack said.

"That's fifteen minutes after class for not paying attention."

"Ugh," Jack grunted, "This sucks..."

"Excuse me, Mr. Javelin?"

"Um, yes, Ma'am, after class. Looking forward to it. Good times, great memories."

The class laughed.

"That's enough! Finish your work," Mrs. Aspen barked.

Heads went down and fingers tapped furiously on tablet screens, but Jack had a hard time focusing. Lately, he felt a bit off, like he was going through life without being a part of it, as if there was a giant piece of It missing, but he could never quite put his finger on what it was.

Of particular note was the strange empty bedroom down the hallway from his own. The octagonal room had been vacant for as long as Jack remembered, but whenever he went to open its door, he'd be crushed by a sudden rush of guilt and sorrow. None of this made any sense to him, after all, it was just an empty room, yet he was inexplicably drawn to it, like a moth to a flame.

Sometimes when his parents were away, he would stand in front of the door for long periods of time trying to work up the courage to open it, but he never could.

"I thought you were in a hurry to get home," Mrs. Aspen's voice shook him from his daydream, "Detention is over. You are free to go."

Jack jumped out of his seat and rushed home to grab his hockey stick and gloves. When he rounded the corner of his street, the neighborhood kids were already deeply engaged in the game.

"Jack, it's about time, we're getting killed out here," Ravi shouted from the net.

"Keep your pants on, dude. Aspen kept me after school. I'm grabbing my stuff. I'll be right back."

The game carried on as the opposing team took several shots on goal in light of his team's lackluster defense.

"C'mon, Jack! They're pounding me! We can really use you out here!"

But Jack wasn't listening. As he approached his house, he was overcome by the feeling of an immense weight pushing down on him. He looked up and saw his reflection, hands pressed against the window of the empty octagonal room, staring down at him. He squeezed his eyes closed and shook his head. When his gaze returned to the window it was empty. He continued to stare up in disbelief, haunted by the vision of what he had just seen.

"Jack, what the hell are you doing!" Ravi demanded, "they're already up 3-zip!"

Jack waved Ravi off, "I said I'm coming..."

He entered the house, walked past his hockey gear, and up the stairs to the mysterious door. He stood meekly in front of it as he had done so many times before, trying to summon the courage to open it. The commotion of the hockey game faded away in the intensity of the moment and the door suddenly clicked and creaked open on its own.

Bright light streamed into the hallway casting Jack as a black silhouette. He stepped through the doorway and confronted the mysterious room for the very first time. His heart pounded heavily, and he was overwhelmed by an intense sense of loss. Jack slumped against the wall and slid down until his head rested between his knees. He sobbed uncontrollably but he did not understand why. As they fell, his tears left craters in the dust on the floor beneath is legs. When he finally got his emotions under control, he raised his head to wipe his tears with his sleeve and there, scrawled into the floor by his feet, were a couple words crossed out with a cracked red X.

The words were hard to make out at first as they were messy and disorganized. He leaned forward onto to his hands and knees in order to get a better look. As he did, the sun emerged from behind a cloud and light streamed through the dusty windows and onto the uneven letters. Jack could make it out now, it read:

the tinker

About The Authors

Evan Gordon is a high school student who spends his time writing, producing, and performing theater. He is co-author of *Souvenirs, Not a High School Show,* a comedic stage play. Evan's writing is influenced by some of his favorite television shows, films and authors, including: James Dashner, Brandon Sanderson, Rick Riordan, Rick Yancey, Star Wars, The Flash, Lost, Stranger Things, and the ultimate, Doctor Who, for which he dreams of writing an episode.

Scott Gordon enjoys playing the ukulele, cartooning, blogging, gardening, and attending ComicCons with his three kids. He has also helped thousands of consumers and businesses switch to clean renewable solar energy and has authored a book on the subject titled: *Divorcing The Electric Company*. His writing influences include: J.R.R. Tolkien, Arthur C. Clarke, Isaac Asimov, George Orwell, Aldous Huxley, Benjamin Hoff, and Daniel Quinn. When not reading sci-fi, Scott enjoys Napoleon Hill, Zig Ziglar, John Wooden, Simon Sinek, and Dan Kennedy.

Other Books in the TinkerVerse

The Tinker and The Fold
Part 1: The Problem with Solaris 3

The Tinker and The Fold
Part 2: The Rise of the Boe

Visit Us Online

Thetinkerandthefold.com

Lagunalanternpublishing.com

Made in the USA
San Bernardino, CA
18 December 2019

61862256R00151